*Winner of the
15th International
Three-Day Novel
Writing Contest . . .*

A Circle
of
Birds

Hayden Trenholm

ANVIL PRESS PUBLISHERS

A CIRCLE OF BIRDS

Copyright © 1993 Hayden Trenholm

Published by Anvil Press
P.O. Box 1575, Station A
Vancouver, B.C., CANADA
V6C 2P7

All rights reserved.

No part of this book may be reproduced in any form or by any means, electronic or mechanical, without permission in writing from the publisher, except by a reviewer, who may quote brief passages in a review to print in a magazine or newspaper or broadcast on radio or television.

This book is a work of fiction. Resemblances to people alive or dead are purely coincidental.

CANADIAN CATALOGUING IN PUBLICATION DATA

TRENHOLM, HAYDEN, 1955-
   A CIRCLE OF BIRDS

   ISBN: 1-895636-03-5
   I. TITLE.

PS8589.R46C5 1993   C813'.54   C93-091262-4
PR9199.3.T73C5 1993

Sections of this book appeared in *sub-TERRAIN Magazine* prior to publication in book form.

Typesetting: Anvil Press.

Cover Design: Don Thompson and Brian Kaufman.

PRINTED AND BOUND IN CANADA.

This book is dedicated to Lynne Malmquist, a source of constant inspiration, feedback and support, without which nothing could be accomplished.

O N E

I

EACH MORNING THERE IS A SCALY SHEATH OF MEMORY LYING ON MY bed, sloughed away during the night. It lies there, glittering in the morning sun. I try to touch it but it crumbles to dust beneath my fingers. It is all slipping away.

The doctors call my condition 'aminesis,' a made-up Greek word that they tell me means death of memory. I keep this posted on the wall beside my bed and refresh myself each morning. Beside this hand-written slogan is a calendar, with the days carefully marked off with a black felt marker I have tied to a string. It is difficult to hold onto the present when your mind is peeling away like the layers of an onion.

The calendar tells me that today is December 31, 1999. This seems to me a day of great portent. I know that tomorrow is not the first day of the twenty-first century. That technically will not occur until next year. But the truth bears little weight against the popular imagination. If most of the world thinks of it as the dawning of the new millennium, why should I or anyone else say them nay?

Today is the last day of 1999. This is of little matter to me as I do not recall anything before 1995. Yesterday, according to my diary, I could remember 1996 quite clearly, but, as I read the words scrawled on the page, the events described could as easily have happened to the man in the moon for all the feelings they evoke in me. It is gone.

Not that 1996 was that memorable. It appears I spent the entire year in the same place as I am now—a hospital bed in the city of Edmonton, Alberta, Canada, Edge of the World. I was not suffering my current affliction. That did not develop until the following year.

At first, the memory loss was tiny. I would forget what I was about to say. This occurs in us all, from time to time. It seems like nothing to worry about. Do not be so sure. As it happened with greater frequency, I began to get worried. So did my doctors. They delayed my release. Then I would lose an entire hour—forget that I had lunch, for example, or gone to the bathroom. This seems silly but it's not. Imagine not being able to remember going to the bathroom for three whole days. You begin to worry. You tell your doctor and he begins to worry. He prescribes an enema. This is an embarrassing procedure to go through when you don't have to.

In 1996, however, my current problems were far away. Then all I had to do was recover from a car accident. This I remember. Today, at least.

II

I watch the car burn, lying on my back on the side of a marshy ditch. Flames reach ten feet in the air as if trying to catch and reclaim the black smoke that rises in oily clumps above it. The light from the fire picks out the scrubby black spruce and bare grey rock on the far side of the ditch. The red-orange flicker sends ghosts running through the trees, howling and gibbering in delight. Blood is trickling down my forehead into my eyes and I try to wipe it away. My right arm does not seem to be working so I have to use my left. As I drag my hand across my face I can see that it is blackened and bruised. Unclean.

Behind me I hear the crunch of wheels on the narrow gravel road. An engine dies and a door opens. I hear voices, tight with fear and disgust. A woman's face comes into view, peering down at me.

"My God, he's still alive," she says. Then she turns away and I can hear the sound of vomiting. A man steps into my line of vision, trying to approach the car. His shape is grotesquely tall and shadowed, surrounded by a halo from the fire. Far above, the aurora borealis cracks and weeps across the northern sky. "There's someone else still in the car," he whispers. "Oh, Jesus, he's still alive." He turns away and I close my eyes.

I AM TIRED. THE DRIVE north from Edmonton to Yellowknife is long and boring. It really shouldn't be done in a single day. Still, it is almost over, only an hour away. Dion is talking, as he has talked for nearly seven hundred miles. I do not normally pick up hitchhikers, but I liked this young man's looks as he stood by the road's edge, waiting.

He is tall, his angular frame both awkward and graceful in every slight movement. His hands stand out most clearly. They are huge and expressive like Michelangelo's David, out of proportion to his body and yet supremely right. His hair is long, well past his shoulders, brown and shining. It frames his broad mobile face like a cassock. He has a clean young face but his eyes are deep and tired. They are the eyes of a very old man, whose life weighs on him and pours out of his heart through his eyes.

"So I concluded," Dion said, his hand tracing a final gesture in the still air, "that all these things they teach you, about God and Heaven and so on, simply made no sense. Look, it's like this. Everything in nature exists in a circle. It rains and the water is absorbed by the earth. The earth gives it up to plants who respire the moisture back into the air, or to lakes where it evaporates. This rises into the air to form clouds and then it rains again. The circle is complete and the rotation starts again. Or the salmon. They are born in one particular stream. They leave, mature, and, when the time comes, return to the same stream to spawn and die. Over and over, we observe the sacred circle.

"Yet most religions assume a linear progression. Christians see a progress of history from creation to Armageddon. Each soul undergoes a similar transmogrification, if that's the word. It is born, it dies and moves on to the next plane of existence, purgatory, heaven or hell, and so on. Even Buddhism, while containing lots of loops back on itself, sees life as a progression of forms and plateaus until Nirvana is achieved. All these religions see existence as a journey from point A to point B, with a beginning and an end, rather than as a trip around a circle, with no point having any more significance than any other."

"There is a danger," I reply, "in oversimplifying things. You cannot simply ascribe certain selected natural cycles to some grander order. People's lives are a journey with a beginning and end. Why shouldn't the spiritual world operate in the same fashion? There are qualitative differences between different categories of things and events."

"Categorization is the product of the rational mind," he says. "An unfortunate bifurcation of the spirit that separates mind from body, heart from soul. Human life is a circle, too. Don't the very old often remind us of the very young? Besides, in each of us are the molecules of thousands of others who died and rotted and returned to the earth."

I look over at him sharply. I wonder how one so young could achieve such certainty about the operations of the universe. The same way I did, I suppose. The car hits a loose patch of gravel, swerves, a wheel catches in a rut at the side of the road. We soar into the air and hang suspended above the ditch, like a dream of flying. Then the car slowly drops, the front end caresses the ground. I am flung forward until the shoulder harness catches me, my head snapping forward onto the wheel. There is a flash of red and black.

I ALWAYS ENJOY CROSSING THE Mackenzie River. It is better in the daytime but even a night time crossing has a special feel. I pull up behind a mud splattered pickup on a wide gravel beach. This serves as a dock for the ferry that shuttles vehicles, a few at a time, across the broad river. Dion gets out of the car and stretches, his arms reaching up to heaven as if in prayer. We missed the boat by only a few minutes and will have to wait for nearly half an hour for its return.

It is pleasant to wait by the side of the river. We are practically alone. The driver of the pickup is grabbing a quick nap. I feel tired myself and would do the same if not for Dion. He walks down to the water's edge and stands staring out at the black water, flowing swiftly but silently north. I follow and stand beside him.

The night is clear and cold. It is late September and a hint of winter has already crept into the air. Across the sky northern lights crackle and laugh, almost blotting out the stars. Dion kneels down in the grey green light and trails his long fingers in the water. He looks up at me and grins.

Across the river, I can see the lights of the ferry as it docks on the far side. Farther up the bank, Fort Providence can be made out through the trees. Everywhere else is darkness. The faint sound of a motor comes from up the river and, as we watch, a single light appears around the long bend of the river and creeps towards the village. "They return," Dion's voice whispers in the darkness, "slow on the leash, pallid the leash-men."

I shiver and return to the car for my jacket. When I come back, Dion has shed his clothing and is swimming in the dark muddy waters of the river. His long white form glows under the shifting sky. He dives deep and I count, one, two, three . . . fourteen, fifteen, before he surfaces far out in the water. I call for him to return, worried that the cold of the water will suddenly clutch at him and pull him under. He waves at me and swims back to shore with strong clean strokes.

He wades back to the beach. His skin glows from within. He grins, then laughs out loud. The driver of the pickup stirs behind us. I take off my jacket and wrap Dion in it, rubbing him roughly to dry and warm his shivering flesh. I turn away as he puts his clothes back on.

"The boat's coming back," I say. "We should go back to the car."

We walk to the car. As we do, he reaches out and claps me on the shoulder. He laughs again. "Your jacket's all wet. Do you have another?" I nod and we get back into the car.

On the boat, we stand leaning against the railing and look out at the dark river. Behind us, the driver of the pickup is washing the mud off his truck with a big hose that lies on the deck for that purpose. When he is done he washes off my car as well. Dion looks down at the white water that roils along the side of the boat.

"Surely you sometimes think about the meaning of it all," he says, continuing the conversation he began as soon as the sun had dropped below the horizon. "In forty years, it must have crossed your mind once or twice."

"Once or twice," I acknowledge. "I'm generally too busy living my life to spend much time contemplating it."

"Good answer." Dion grins. "Stock answer number seventeen, I think. Somewhat worn but still solid, reliable."

I turn away and walk to the front of the boat to watch it dock. The air is cool against my face and I can faintly smell the grey velvet odour of the bush. I close my eyes and feel the vibration of the boat and Dion's hand on my back.

I TURN OFF THE YELLOWHEAD onto Route Forty-Three that becomes the Mackenzie Highway. Not far past the junction there is a long straight stretch that gently climbs a hill. Half way up the hill where the road widens slightly, a person is standing, a pack at their feet, a small sign clutched in their hand. I think at first it is a woman. I suppose it is the long hair or the taut grace of the body, poised like a dancer on the shoulder of the road. As I approach I see it is a young man.

I slow the car and pull over. A quiet voice assures me this is all right. His sign says Yellowknife. Axe murderers do not hitchhike to Yellowknife. I reach over and open the door. He runs up to the car, leans forward and peers through the frame, assessing me. He grins, throws his pack over the seat into the back and hops in.

He sticks out his hand for me to shake. His huge hand engulfs mine, his warm strong fingers squeeze gently and release. It is the kind of quick strong handshake that always feels right between strangers. It does not linger too long nor is it limp and hesitant. It is a handshake that says here I am. It is a handshake that speaks of certainty and warmth but imposes nothing, asks nothing.

"Hi. My name is Dion." Dion, nothing more. This is an introduction meant to last the length of a ride, no more. This voice is melodious, a poet's voice. His eyes stare directly at mine. They are wide-set and deep. It is like looking into a well.

"I'm David." I don't know why I lie to him. "I'm pleased to meet you, Dion."

"David?" He smiles at me. "You don't look much like a David. More like an Arthur or a Jeremy."

"What does an Arthur look like?" I ask.

"Hard to say. Something like you. Grey at the temples, a beard. A chiselled English look. Davids don't have beards and their looks are always more European. I've made a study of this."

I look straight ahead. Traffic is light and we move swiftly down the highway. Dion is a treasure trove of ideas, theories and opinions. He shares them freely. I find myself listening to him the way you listen to the radio when you are driving. His voice is musical and mellifluous. The words are less important than the tone.

On either side of the road farmers are harvesting their crops. It has been a dream year for farmers. It rained hard through May and June. July and August were hot and sunny, with a day or two of gentle rain scattered throughout. September remained mild, no frosts to disturb the delicate wheat and canola. To the south, through the American West, there had been hail and terrible wind storms in August. In Russia they had snow. Europe suffered the worst outbreak of rust they had ever seen. People are hungry everywhere. Canadian farmers have never been happier.

Dion's voice rings with a rich harvest song. He talks about birds and about the meaning of dreams. At times, he drones like a combine, echoing the faint roar of motors that comes through the window of the car. Then he sighs like the sound of wheat falling beneath a thresher. His voice matches the slow progress north.

As we pass beyond the farms and come to the first hint of the Northern Shield, his voice changes, deepens, ageing like the ancient rocks that thrust themselves to the surface.

"I began my journey two years ago," he tells me. "I'm almost done. After Yellowknife, there is only the Yukon and Alaska. I've been to every province in Canada, every state of America and Mexico. I have completely consumed North America in my dreams."

We cross the border as the sun touches the horizon. I stop the car so Dion can get out. He walks along the road and then turns into the bush at the side of the road. I fall asleep and dream of fire.

III

Each moment now, memory is slipping away, eaten up by the chemical monster that has come to live in my brain. I scribble the word, Dion, into my diary. I stare at it. I do not know what it means. I look at the word, aminesis, scrawled on the wall. It means nothing to me.

I look down at my hands. It seems to me that they should be larger. Maybe they were once. Along my right hand is a long scar that runs from my index finger up the back of my hand almost to my elbow. I wonder how I got it.

I get up from my bed. I notice that I am limping. This strikes me as somewhat odd. I do not recall having a limp.

I am in a hospital room. I recognize it only because all hospitals look the same. I go to the bathroom but I do not need to urinate. I stand for the longest time at the bowl with my penis in my hand but nothing comes. This worries me. After a while I put it back into my pyjamas. I start to cry.

I turn around. An old face, with a faint scar across its forehead stares at me from the mirror. It is my father's face, right before he died. I scream.

They come running into the room and help me back to the bed. Two nurses and a doctor push me down. The doctor takes out a needle and shoves it in my arm. I struggle against the drug that pours into my veins. I know somehow that sleep is my enemy.

TWO

I

He looked at the circle of older boys who stared back at him eagerly. Sam, the leader of the gang, shoved the can of gasoline toward him.

"Go on," Sam said, "you want to be part of the Flame Throwers, you have to do it. Or are you chicken?"

The other boys began to make clucking sounds, sticking their thumbs into their armpits to make stubby wings. They poked their heads forward in imitation of hens pecking at grain. Their cackles became laughter.

Billy grabbed the can and started to raise it to his lips. He hesitated and set it down again, blushing hard. The laughs and taunts grew louder and threatened to drown him. Tears began in his eyes and he squeezed them hard and looked away to hide them from the others.

"Here," said Albert, the youngest of the boys, "I'll show you how, one more time. It's easy." Sam glared at Albert but nodded his head. Billy smiled his thanks. Albert was two years older than him but small. He had forced his way into the club the summer before, proving himself in a dozen scraps to be the equal of the other boys. It was he who had championed Billy's initiation.

Albert raised the gas can to his lips and took a long mouthful, holding it in his bulging cheeks while he dug a wooden match out of his dungaree pocket. He set the gas can far back against the wall and struck the match on the floor of the barn. He held the burning stick at arm's length and fired the gasoline in a steady smooth stream from his mouth. The clear liquid arched to a point just above the top of the flame and a fireball blossomed in the air.

The fire streamed back along the trail of fuel towards Albert's face. At the last moment he clamped his lips tight together in a sharp whistling spit. The quick exhalation carried the flame away from his mouth to be consumed in the torch that hovered above his hand. Albert quickly pulled his arm down and away so that none of the flaming liquid splattered on his hand as it fell to the barn floor. The other boys jumped up and stamped the remaining flames out with their feet, smothering the last of it in an old horse blanket. Their laughter echoed through the rafters of the old barn that sat on the edge of the abandoned MacAfee farm.

Albert got up and retrieved the gas can. He handed it solemnly to Billy. He reached once more into his pants and pulled out another of the long wooden matches that they had stolen from Mr. Anderson's general store down at the crossroads.

Billy took the gas can and looked once more into the grinning faces of the other boys. He raised it to his lips and took the acrid fluid into his mouth. It burned his lips and tongue. He almost choked on the fumes that filled his nose and throat. Sam took the can from him and moved it well out of harm's way. He nodded and Billy struck the match on a rusty protruding nail.

He stared at the flame that hovered above his outstretched hand. It seemed enormous and far away. He did not think he could spit the gas that far. He cocked his head and then thrust it forward, spraying the gas from his lips with all the air in his lungs. Even as it hit the flame the other boys were rising. Billy knew he had done it wrong.

The fire burst back from the match and struck him hard in the face. Through the flames and the black oily smoke he could see that his entire right arm was ablaze. He could hear the boys shouting with fear and horror. Sam and Albert grabbed him and threw him onto the floor, wrapping the old blanket around him and rolling him over and over to douse the flames.

II

He lay on his back in the damp straw, wondering how he had gotten there. He lifted his right hand and held it in front of his face. It was burned, almost black in places, great patches of skin were sloughing off the back of his hand and his fingers like that of a snake. He wondered if he would lose his hand. One of the boys turned away and was sick.

He felt hot and he tossed restlessly. He must have slept, for when he opened his eyes again the sun was nearly at the horizon. His sister was sitting beside him.

"Oh Billy, what have you done now?" Her voice was tight with concern. She placed a cool cloth on his forehead and gave him a drink of something, water and honey, he thought. It was cool and slightly sweet.

She took his burned hand in hers. He winced in pain but did not cry out. She carefully washed it in a pan of cool water.

"It's not as bad as it looks," she said. "It's only the skin that's been burnt away, the flesh and bone is intact. Move your hand for me."

His fingers felt stiff and it hurt badly to wriggle them but he did as he was told. Diana smiled down at him and stroked his cheek. That hurt too but he didn't turn away. She turned her attention back to his hand, gently coating it in salve that she scooped from a big jar. Then she wrapped it loosely in white cloth.

"You look sunburned," she said, after a bit. "Your face is red and," she laughed, "all the hair is gone, your eyebrows, your lashes, your bangs, even from inside your nose."

Billy slept again. He was roused by Diana's hand on his shoulder. "We should go home," she whispered. "It's getting late. Can you walk?"

Billy got to his feet. He felt a little shaky but he followed his sister out of the barn and onto the narrow path that led to the Jacobs' farm. He and Diana had been sent there to help with the harvest. The couple had no children of their own and could not afford to hire hands from town. Instead they took on children from their neighbours, whom they paid with a portion of their crop and a few dollars in cash. This was the first summer that Billy had been judged big enough to be sent out to work.

Billy knew that Mr. Jacobs would be angry with him, both for missing the day's work and for hurting his hand. It would be hard for him to do his chores in the days ahead. Billy wondered if he would beat him. If it were his own father there would be little doubt of the hiding he would get, but Mr. Jacobs seldom even raised his voice to the children who worked for him, let alone his hand.

They walked slowly up to the farmhouse. There was an automobile parked in front of the house. Billy gaped in wonder and delight at the shiny black shape with its large spoked wheels. He had heard there were several in town. He had seen pictures of automobiles before in the magazines his mother got from Boston but had never been this close to one in real life. He reached out his hand to touch it as they went by.

Through the front window he could see Mr. Jacobs sitting at the dining table, poring over papers with a man Billy did not know. Mrs. Jacobs was playing the upright piano in the corner of the room. Billy could see her mouth open and close as she sang hymns.

Diana led him around to the back door and they entered as quietly as they could through the kitchen. They crept up the back stairs towards the attic room they shared with the three Trueman children. Before they reached the top of the first flight they were stopped by the sound of Mr. Jacobs' deep voice.

"William. Diana. Where have you been?" he called.

"Billy was down in the woodlot, chopping wood, like you asked him," Diana responded.

"Don't lie to me, child," Jacobs said mildly. "I went down to the woodlot myself this afternoon. Billy wasn't there and from the looks of things hadn't been there all day. Now come down here, boy, and speak for yourself." Diana began to follow him down the stairs. "You go on up to bed, girl," Jacobs stopped her. "I'll deal with you in the morning." Diana squeezed her brother's shoulder before turning away to do as she was told. Billy slowly made his way down the stairs.

As he stepped into the light of the lantern that Jacobs held in his hand, Billy slipped his bandaged hand behind his back and looked down to try to hide his face. The farmer reached out and grasped the boy's chin roughly in his hand and turned it up. "Look at me when I'm talking to you, boy." Billy cried out in pain at the rough calloused fingers on his burned cheeks. Jacobs pulled back his hand as if stung.

The man dropped to one knee and peered into the boy's face, taking in the rough red patches of burned skin and the absent hair. He gently brought Billy's hand from behind his back and looked at the white bandage.

"How did this happen, Billy?" Jacobs' voice was as low and soft as a woman's. "You can tell me the truth. I won't hurt you."

In a moment he forgot all the promises he had made to the other boys. His vows of silence meant nothing before the soft sad eyes that held him in their gaze. He blurted out the story of the Flame Throwers and their fiery rites as swiftly and as hotly as he had earlier spewed out gasoline. When he had finished Jacobs took Billy in his arms and hugged him.

"You go up and sleep in the front room, Billy," he said at last. "You may sleep badly tonight and I don't want you disturbing the other children. We'll talk again in the morning."

Billy slowly climbed the stairs to the second floor. His sister was sitting on the ladder leading up to the attic. He smiled wordlessly and nodded toward the front bedroom. She blew him a kiss goodnight and climbed the ladder to her bed.

Billy made his way slowly down the dark hallway, feeling his way carefully with his left hand. He reached the doorway at the end of the hall and pushed open the door. Moonlight streamed through the window that overlooked the yard. Billy went to it and looked down on the strange machine that still sat before the house. From the grate in the floor he could faintly hear the tinkle of music and the low murmur of men's voices.

This room was a mystery. No one lived in it, and never had, according to Jim Trueman, the eldest Trueman boy, who had been coming here for three summers. Once when he returned early from his chores he had seen Mrs. Jacobs through the open door, sitting on the bed, rocking and singing to herself. Now here he was. He went back to the door and closed it until he heard the soft click of the latch.

He crossed to the narrow bed that lay along one wall and stripped off his clothes. He felt hot and lay on top of the blankets, his white body pale against the darkness. The bed had a faint musty smell.

Billy stirred, pushing against his dreams. At first, he was afraid. He was covered in fire, rushing down his arm to wrap his body in fierce flames. Then that was gone and he was swimming in the stream that flowed between the Jacobs and MacAfee farms. The stream spread wider and wider until it became a river. He swam and dove in the dark brown water like a fish. He dove deep and when he swam back to the surface he broke through it and rose into the air until he was flying high above the farm. He looked down on the farm as he made a big circle around it in the air and in the circle he could see the cycle of seasons, changing from fall to winter and on to spring then summer. He thought of how pleasant it would be to live his whole life here with Mr. and Mrs. Jacobs.

Next he was driving in the automobile with the strange dark-clothed man he had seen through the window. They drove down the long gravel road towards town, driving faster and faster, the farms streaming past. The man was talking but Billy couldn't make out what he was saying. His voice sounded like the organ at the church, steady droning music that threatened to plunge him back into the river.

The dark man leaned over in the car seat and hovered over him. He reached out his hand and put it on Billy's chest. The hand slid down his body where he was lying on the dark blankets and it touched him across his stomach and down lower, between his legs, touching and squeezing him. The dark man leaned over him and

Billy could smell the sweet-sour odour of his breath on his face and felt his mouth against his skin.

Billy shuddered awake on the bed. He was shivering in the cool draft of air that flowed through the half-open door. He looked at the door, the thicker darkness of the hallway pouring through the opening into the room. He got up and pushed the door shut until he heard the click of the latch. He went back to the bed and pulled back the blankets and crawled between them. His hand throbbed and he lay it across his chest on top of the blanket. As he fell asleep he heard his father's voice shouting at him to run away.

III

After three days, Billy's hand was well enough for him to resume his lighter chores around the house. Mr. Jacobs did not say anything further about the Flame Throwers, nor did he tell the boys' fathers about their club. It was clear to Billy though that he was not to go again to the MacAfee barn. He accepted this without question or resentment.

The man with the automobile was introduced as Reverend Scott, a travelling preacher who had come, as he put it, "to reclaim the heathen Nova Scotians for Jesus." He was from the same church as the Jacobs and so could claim their hospitality but Billy did not think that he and Mr. Jacobs got along very well. Most nights he could hear them arguing late into the night.

Billy continued to sleep in the front room although his hand no longer kept him awake at night. He missed his sister sleeping in the bed beside him but he did not complain, for every night before bed he could look down on the wondrous machine at the front of the house and imagine riding in it.

Most nights he slept soundly but sometimes he was wakened by the same strange dream. Always it started in the automobile.

Sometimes, the dark man was driving and sometimes he was behind the wheel himself. They were driving down the road past farmers who stood in the fields staring at them. Sometimes the fields were on fire and sometimes there were great flocks of flame-coloured birds hovering over the fields getting ready to sweep down and eat the crops. Then the dark man would lean over and touch him with his mouth, run his long tongue down over his skin.

Billy reached down in the darkness of half sleep. He felt very strange. He reached down and his thing was hard and it was covered with a warm sticky liquid. He thought he must be bleeding and he sat up in bed afraid and panting. His breath was harsh in his ears and he almost cried out but stopped himself. In the moonlight he could see he was not bleeding and he knew what had happened. He had seen animals like this and remembered that Jim had told him that this happens to all boys at a certain time though Jim was vague as to why. Billy lay down and wondered what it meant that he always dreamt about the dark man in the automobile.

After another week they took the bandage off his hand. He would be returning home in a few days and he preferred not to have to explain the bandage to his father. The flesh of his hand was pink and two of his fingers were stiff with scarred flesh. In time the scars would darken and fade and with luck his father might believe his hand had always looked like that. Billy asked Mr. Jacobs not to tell his father about the burn and the man had only turned his face away from Billy and grunted. Then he stood and stared out the front window for the longest time as if he had forgotten the boy standing there. Then he turned and looked at Billy. His wide-set grey eyes were deep and watery like looking down a well. He nodded at the boy and sent him from the room.

That night Billy had his dream again about the dark man. He woke up, his bare chest cold where a tongue had streaked wetly across it. Two black forms were struggling above him, shouting in deep voices so Billy was afraid. They fell through the doorway into the hall with a crash. The door swung shut and Billy was alone.

Outside, a man was cursing in a deep angry voice. There was the sound of running feet on the stairs and a woman's scream. The automobile roared to life in the yard below.

In the morning Reverend Scott was gone. Mrs. Jacobs was in the parlour crying, holding a Bible and a small doll in her lap. Jacobs put Billy into his wagon and took him back to his father's farm.

THREE

I

My eyes snap open and stare up at the white ceiling. Crisp white sheets are stretched across my chest and arms so that at first I cannot move. I turn my head toward the wall and look at the poster there. Aminesis—the death of memory. I turn in the other direction. There is a man in a white doctor's coat sitting in a chair, looking at a chart. He is dark with straight black hair.

"Donde estoy?" I ask.

"What?" he replies, in English.

"Bueno, habla ingles." I smile at him.

"I'm afraid I don't . . . " He has an English accent.

"Was I in an accident?" I ask.

"Not recently. You were upset. We gave you a sedative. Don't you remember?" He stops. "Oh, I am sorry."

I stare at the ceiling. In the whorls of the plaster I see a face staring back, framed in long brown hair. His wide-set grey eyes are laughing. It can be a terrible shock to see Jesus staring at you from your hospital ceiling, even in Mexico, where such occurrences are commonplace. I try to remember how I got here.

II

The bus is lying on its side in the jungle. I look back at the road, twenty metres up the side of the hill. There is a brown gash through the deep green of the jungle where the bus has swept away the vegetation as it slid down the ravine. Two parrots are flying in a circle above the crushed transport, screaming at us. Many of the passengers are screaming back.

Everything is a mess. There is blood everywhere. The driver is dead. He is probably better off since they prosecute bus drivers for accidents in Mexico. Better to be dead than spend twenty years in a Mexican jail. I know he is dead because I am sitting three rows back and his head is sitting in my lap. The rest of him is still wedged behind the wheel. I set the head on the seat next to me and sit for a moment staring at it as it stares back at me. I reach over and try to close his eyes like they do in the movies but they won't stay shut. It is a bit unnerving. I probably wouldn't take it so well if I weren't still high.

Beside me in the seat is Julia. I think she is dead too, although her body is unmarked. Her head is lying at an unnatural angle on her shoulder so I presume her neck is broken. I know she is very flexible but I don't think she's flexible enough to do that. Her head looks funny so I laugh.

I feel the acid move behind my eyes and the scene rearranges. Everything looks artificial. All the Mexicans have that oddly distorted look that you often see in the paintings of Diego Rivera. I wonder briefly if he ever took acid but decide not. It's not a Marxist thing to do.

I push my way past Julia through the twisted frame of the window. In doing so, I have to drag myself across her body. Her blouse rips open and I look down on her big nearly perfect breasts. My cock which is now pressed against one of her tits starts to get hard in my pants, but then I twist and I feel a sharp pain run through my ribs and my cock goes limp again. I forget about Julia and struggle through the window. All I can think is that the bus might catch on fire. I am sweating with fear until I remember that the bus runs on diesel and it takes a lot to set that stuff on fire. I flop down on the jungle floor and look up at the parrot flying overhead. It looks huge and misshapen and I realize it is an airplane flying low over the crash.

The ground under me seems to be moving. I look down and see that I am lying on a huge carpet of insects. This does not bother me for I know that insects are our friends and that they have come to help me. Only when they start to lift me up so I am floating over the ground do I begin to get disturbed. I try to get up and there is a terrible shooting pain in my chest and I black out.

BEFORE WE GET ON THE bus at San Cristobal de Las Casas, we both drop a tab of acid. I haven't done acid in a very long time, nearly twenty years, in fact. I doubt I would be doing it now if it weren't for Julia.

She looks over at me and smiles. Her teeth are very white in her tanned face. She has very blue eyes, like the sea off Cozomel. "Are you ready to travel, David?" This is the name I always use when I am uncertain of where I stand.

I smile back and help her onto the bus. I check our tickets and guide us to the third row behind the driver. Julia finds the idea of assigned seating on a bus amusing. The bus fills up. We are the only gringos and people look at us curiously as they board.

Before the bus pulls out of the station about a dozen people get on board selling tortillas or fruit or hats to keep off the sun. Mexicans are the true entrepreneurs of North America. Everybody is in business, everything is for sale. Americans, who are used to more regulated commerce, find this disturbing and a little disgusting. Some day the Mexicans will eat them alive.

A man selling Tiger Balm is the last one to get on the bus. He stands at the front of the aisle and extols the virtues of his product in Spanish far too rapid for my limited skills. I catch a word here and there—*medicina maravillosa*—and understand that it will cure whatever ails you.

I explain to Julia and she has to have some. She beckons him over and bargains, very badly. He grins broadly at her from beneath a thick black mustache before handing over a small pot in exchange for fifteen thousand pesos. "Muy bonita, senorita." He grins at me and turns to leave. As he goes I see him gesture to the driver and laugh. "Tetas maravillas, non?"

"Chinganda verdad, amigo."

I laugh and look at Julia's breasts. Fucking right. The bus driver looks back to see that everyone is sitting down and pulls out of the stall. The bus belches and a black oily cloud of smoke reaches into the air above the station as he steers slowly onto the rough cobbled street that leads out to the highway.

San Cristobal is over two thousand metres above sea level but before descending down into the jungles around Panlenque we must first climb another five hundred metres or so over the crest of the mountains that run down the spine of America from Alaska to Argentina. The country here is dry and lightly forested, the trees interspersed with tall cacti. The valleys are full of scrawny cattle and herds of scruffy-looking goats. Part way up the mountain lies a military base surrounded by a tall barbed wire fence.

This country looks odd enough at the best of times but as the acid begins to take effect, it all starts to look like a painting by Dali. I remember this now. When I take drugs, I feel I am in an art gallery. Most people look to me like they stepped out of a painting by El Greco, their faces too long and dressed in dark and sombre shades. This varies of course with place, time and mood. When I am lucky, Rubens dominates and everyone glows and looks fat and happy.

This is pleasant. I look out the window for a while at the drooping cacti and the cattle who seem to stare back at me with deep grey intelligent eyes. I look over at Julia and wonder if she is really sitting there with her clothes off, masturbating while the Mexicans watch and clap their hands in time. I start to get a hard-on which surprises me because we made love five times the night before. I grin and feel my teeth moving around and this bothers me for a while but then it goes away and, when I look over again, Julia is fast asleep with her head tilted at the most impossible angle and the bus is flying.

There are moments when you feel you are plummeting toward some particular point in space and time, that some hand is guiding your every faltering backward step toward some unalterable destiny. This is one of those moments and then the bus hits the side of the ravine.

IT IS A LONG TIME since I felt the body of a horse hard between my legs. Our guide leads us along a narrow trail that leads from San Cristobal to Chamula. You can drive there along the road in a little more than thirty minutes, but what's the point? Our route is shorter but will take nearly three hours. The horses are well trained and used to this route. They have probably travelled it a hundred times. I have to work hard to make mine do anything it doesn't want to do. I enjoy the challenge.

I look over at the young American woman on the chestnut mare. I met her two days ago in one of the few bars in San Cristobal that has dancing. I taught her the tango, much to the delight of the salsa band that seldom was asked to play anything so exotic and traditional, especially by a turisto. She is probably the most beautiful woman I have ever seen, certainly the most beautiful woman I have ever slept with. She is twenty-two but, thankfully, prefers older men. I undress in the dark so she cannot see the ravages of thirty-eight years of hard living. She doesn't seem to care that I am not thin and hard like the young men she was sitting with when I asked her to dance. Still, I feel better in the dark.

As we get farther from town, it is like riding back into the past. We cross a narrow foot bridge over a stream where dark Mayan women are washing bright woollen blankets. Men look up from behind ox-drawn ploughs as we pass. Everywhere the fields are terraced as the people try to draw the last drop of wealth from the recalcitrant land. Along the trail, next to streams, narrow valleys and paths leading up into the mountains, there are white double-barred crosses, the upper bar narrower and shorter than the lower one. These are not Christian symbols but Mayan markers of holy and mystical places. Julia wants to stop and have her picture taken in front of one but the guide puts his hand in front of the camera and forbids it.

When we reach Chamula, the guide leaves us while he tends the horses. I buy him a Corona. He thanks me and lies in the shade to sip it slowly and wait for us. We go into the village hall and buy our tickets to visit the church, which is the main attraction of the village. *"No pictura, no pictura!"* they shout as we leave the office, so we give them our cameras to hold for us.

Julia and I cross the square to the churchyard that is marked off by a low stone wall. Outside the wall, women lurk and they rush up to us holding out belts and small clay dolls dressed in brilliantly dyed bits of cloth. They tie the belts around our waists and press the dolls into our hands. I finally buy one of each to satisfy them but it has the opposite effect. One sale is made, why not another? The moment we step into the churchyard they leave us alone.

The church looks much like any other church you might see in Mexico. White stucco rectangle with a tall bell tower in front, above wide, wooden double doors. A man sitting in the dust outside takes our tickets and assures himself that we have no hidden cameras. He motions us to silence and waves us through.

It is dark and cool inside the church. The first thing I notice is the wailing of women, a high fluting call in Mayan. There is no Spanish spoken here. There are no pews or seats of any kind. People are standing or, more often, kneeling on the thick rushes strewn across the stone paved floor. There are hundreds, maybe thousands, of candles burning, lighting everything from below. A few are at the front of the church by the altar where a huge cross is lying on its side against the wall. At first, I think the nave has been desecrated but then I realize this is a cross that is used in outdoor ceremonies and is only being stored here. The altar has no cross.

Most of the candles sit in front of huge statues of saints that line both walls of the church. Each saint has its own cadre of worshippers, bringing offerings and prayers for their attention. I have been told that each saint has been linked to an ancient Mayan god. The veneer is Catholic but the religion is not. Until this moment I did not believe it. Now I know that no priest rules here.

We stand barely inside the doors of the church. I feel as if a hand is laid on my shoulder as soon as we enter, preventing me from going any further. To my right, two men are standing with a young boy. They are passing a bottle between them. The first man takes a drink. He takes a second mouthful and spits it cleanly onto the floor in a smooth arch of liquid sailing above the flames of the candles. He passes the bottle to the second man who repeats the action. They give the bottle to the boy who takes it but then hesitates. The men nod their encouragement. The boy takes a mouthful of liquid and swallows it. He puts the bottle to his mouth once more, then sprays the fluid messily onto the floor. He wipes his face where the liquid has dribbled down his chin and looks away. One of the men laughs and rubs the boy's head. Julia laughs and the man looks at us, his wide-set grey eyes cutting right through us.

We do not say a word but turn and leave the church and stand gasping in the hot bright air of the churchyard.

III

"Estoy en Mexico! Estoy en Mexico!" I shout, as if speaking in Spanish will make it true.

The doctor tells me that I am not in Mexico but in Edmonton. I ask him what the fuck would I be doing in Edmonton. I haven't even been in Canada for two years. He tells me I've been in this hospital for four years, that it is 1999 not 1993. I tell him he is a liar.

I am lying on a bed. There is a strange man in a doctor's white coat standing over me. He has a dark complexion and straight dark hair. I have no idea who he is.

There are moments when you feel that there must be a purpose to everything, that there is some pattern that must be grasped. You feel that if you could only reach out your hand and grab that pattern, everything would be clear and you would know who you are and where and why. I reach out my hand to grasp the ring on the merry-go-round but when I do it crumbles to dust beneath my fingers. It is all slipping away.

FOUR

I

BILL SHIFTED ON THE SWAYING WOODEN FLOOR, TRYING TO FIND A more comfortable position. During the night his knapsack had twisted under him and now the point of his heavy leather boot was sticking in the small of his back. The low morning sun flickered through fenceposts onto his face as the train rolled through the flat empty land.

At the end of the car, a man began to cough. The coughing went on for some minutes. Another voice began to curse harshly. Bill opened his gluey eyes and peered around.

The car looked the same as it had since he boarded it in Nova Scotia, perhaps a few less bodies than before. Some men had gotten off in Manitoba and more when the train crossed the border into Saskatchewan. Bill thought he might ride all the way to Calgary, where the harvest excursion came to an end.

At the far end of the train a fight broke out between the coughing man and the one who sat cursing at him. Scottie, the burly ex-policeman from Stellarton, leapt up from his spot halfway down the car and laid into the combatants with the thick wooden truncheon he always kept by his side. The coughing man pulled out a knife and cut Scottie across the cheek. Scottie smashed his club onto the man's wrist and Bill could hear the snap of bone as the knife skittered across the floor and disappeared into someone's pocket. The club came down on the coughing man's head and he went down in a heap and lay moaning quietly to himself, clutching his wrist. Bill closed his eyes and went back to sleep.

An hour later the porter came through the car wheeling a trolley with a kettle filled with sticky oatmeal and a basket of stale buns. These he sullenly doled out to the men who lined each side of the railcar. The men had to supply their own bowls and those who had none would take the oatmeal in their cupped hands or their hats. After five days, the car stank from rotting food that had slipped between fingers and been ground into the oily wood of the floor.

Bill took his cup of cold thin cereal onto the platform between the cars, away from the sour smells of sweat and vomit, away from the sweet cloying stench from the honey-closet at the end of the car. He preferred the oily black smoke streaming from the twin locomotives to the stink of his fellow travellers. Others had the same idea and the landing was crowded. Bill managed to wedge himself against the far door so the cool prairie wind blew in his face. He ate in silence and tried to ignore the crude voices that whispered and laughed and the unwashed bodies pressed tight against him.

One by one the other men drifted back into the railcar until only Bill and one other stood on the platform. He hoped the other man would leave. He had to piss and wanted to do it over the side of the platform. His bladder was so full he had a hard-on. He shifted his weight from side to side and waited. The other man was older, his shaggy hair and unkempt beard streaked with grey. He peered at Bill with watery eyes. He fixed his gaze on Bill's crotch and Bill turned away. The man made a sucking sound with his mouth and when Bill looked at him he made an ugly gesture and licked his lips. Bill stepped towards the door of the car.

The man put his hand on Bill's shoulder and whispered something but he could not quite make out the words. Bill turned and put his right hand on the man's chest. He slid it slowly down and across the soft belly, down across the hardness in his pants. The man grunted and smiled as Bill pushed his hand between his legs. He reached up and squeezed hard so the man gasped and leaned forward in pain, reaching out with both hands to grab Bill's arm and push it away. When he did, Bill swung his left arm up so his forearm smashed into the man's face. The older man's head snapped back and Bill followed through until his elbow smacked into the man's eye. He went down against the far corner of the platform.

Bill entered the railcar and felt sick as he walked back to where his pack lay. The car was swaying and black dots danced before his eyes. A quiet voice told him it was time to get off the train. Bill pulled his boots from his pack and put them on. Then he closed the pack and sat on the floor with the pack in his lap. After a while the grey-haired man came back into the car. His nose was twisted out of shape and blood had streamed down and stained his beard a rusty red, hiding the streaks of grey. The man glared sullenly at Bill and went to sit at the far end of the car next to the coughing man.

Bill could hear the low murmur of voices and saw the grey-haired man gesture toward him several times. Finally Bill got up, grabbed his pack and went back onto the platform and had a piss over the side of the train. When he was done he went through the door into the next car and then on to the one after that and found an empty spot on the floor where he could sit. When the train stopped at a small town just east of Regina, Bill got off. He went to the table where the farmers' representative was sitting and signed up to work at the farm on the top of the list. An hour later he was sitting in the back of a wagon going south.

II

The harvest had gone well the year before. Everyone thought 1929 would be a good year. That winter was cold and dry, little snow and a steady north wind that leeched the moisture out of the ground and blew the dusty soil in swirling circles over the farms. The spring rains were late and when they finally came they were too hard. The dry ground couldn't hold the water and it tore great strips of soil down from the hills and into the rivers to be washed away forever. The summer was hot and dry. It didn't rain on the Thompson farm for over four months. The few stunted crops that had sprouted, had withered and died. In the fall the market crashed and the banks began to grow desperate. Loans were called and those who could not pay lost their farms.

Ira Thompson was a frugal man. He had carefully saved his money during the relatively good years of the previous decade. He kept his farm from the bank and then watched it slowly blow away in the wind.

Bill stayed on at the farm even after Ira could no longer pay his wages. He did his chores in exchange for meals. When there were no more chores to do in the dying fields he sought work in town and turned his meagre pay over to Ira to support the family.

In November he married Ira's daughter, Sarah. He wrote his father to tell him of his marriage. Two months later he received a cable. "Your mother dying. Come home." He carefully folded the telegram into a small square and put it in one corner of his wallet where he kept it for the next twenty-five years.

Sarah was no raving beauty but Bill didn't care. He didn't care that she was ten years his elder or that her left leg was slightly twisted and weak from a childhood brush with polio. None of these things mattered. Sarah made him feel almost complete for the first time in his life. Almost.

They would go for long walks through dusty fields or along dried-up stream beds. There was an old abandoned barn at the far end of the farm where they would go on Sunday afternoons in fall before the weather turned cold. They would lie naked between thick blankets spread in the straw and make love. Bill loved the feeling of Sarah's wide full mouth against his and her small hard breasts pressed against his chest. When he lay inside her with the sunlight dappled across them he could forget about everything. Forget the empty hollow that nestled inside him, forget the restless voice that kept talking to him about fire, forget the dark face that hovered just on the edge of his vision. For one brief instant, as he came inside her, it would all go away. But then it would come back. Then he would lie in Sarah's arms and cry while she held him and stroked his hair and looked at him with her sad wide-set grey eyes.

When they were married in November, Sarah was already two months pregnant. Through the winter Bill delighted in running his hand across her swelling stomach. He would place his head against her belly and listen. They would sit naked in front of the fire in the small house that Bill and Ira had made from an old shed and part of the abandoned barn. Bill would tell Sarah his dreams. Sometimes he would tell her his nightmares. Then she would kiss his eyes and smile at him and day by day the pain began to fade until by spring it was only a faint memory.

The pregnancy was not an easy one. Sarah was often sick but she never complained. Toward the end she found it hard to walk on her weak leg and Bill would bring her meals in bed and would even bathe her and brush her hair when she felt too tired to do it herself. To Bill, she looked more and more beautiful as the time for her labour approached. Somehow he could not see the hollows in her cheeks and the dark circles beneath her eyes.

Ira watched his daughter as she grew bigger and weaker under the burden of the new life inside her. He tightened his belt further and found money for the hospital. When Sarah's water broke he and Bill drove her into town, the old truck whining and creaking as it careened wildly down the narrow gravel roads. Farmers picking at their dusty fields stopped and stared at them as they passed.

Bill held Sarah in his arms as Ira drove. She was babbling in a high keening voice, her eyes wide with pain. He could not understand what she was saying. Bill was flying across dark gravel roads, a dark man behind the wheel, a voice in his ears. He was flying toward some unalterable destiny. He swallowed hard.

The car screamed to a halt in front of the small hospital. Bill half-carried Sarah up the steps to the entrance where a nurse met them with a wheelchair. The nurse wheeled Sarah down the hall, leaving Bill to watch helplessly after her. He could hear Sarah frantically calling out his name as she disappeared through the two wide doors at the end of the hall.

After a bit, Bill got up and went out and sat on the front steps. He lit a cigarette and sat smoking it slowly. Ira came and sat beside him and Bill gave him the cigarette. Ira took it and had a smoke. He looked at Bill and Bill looked at him. The smoke was curling up from Ira's mouth and hung about his head like a halo with the sun shining through. They did not say anything but after a while Ira put his hand on Bill's shoulder. Then he got up and walked back to the truck and sat in it staring straight ahead.

Bill got up and walked around the block and when he got back Ira was leaning against the truck looking like a man who had just had his guts kicked out. When Bill looked at him, Ira turned away.

Bill ran up the hospital steps and down the hall. The doctor met him at the end of the hall and put his hand in the middle of Bill's chest to stop him. Bill felt an electric shock run across his chest, down his belly to his thighs.

He stared into the doctor's face. The doctor turned away.

"The baby was born dead. I'm sorry." His voice was gravelly.

"Sarah?"

"I don't know. It doesn't look good."

"Is she going to die?"

"We're doing everything we can."

The doctor went back through the double doors. Bill slumped against the wall, his legs crumpling beneath him. A voice was screaming in his ear and a dark man was laughing and Bill was falling toward a single point of light.

After an hour they let him into the room to see Sarah. He took her hand and she smiled up at him.

"I can't see you, Bill," she said. "I can't see your face."

Bill leaned over Sarah and touched her cheek, but her grey eyes looked right through him and beyond him at someone else. He took his hand away.

Sarah did not speak again for a long time and Bill stood up and looked toward the door where the doctor waited outside. Then Sarah coughed and her hand moved a little. The point of light became larger and brighter and then Sarah's voice came from a long way off and smothered it a bit.

"Don't give into him, Bill," Sarah said. "Fall in love again and don't give into him."

"I don't want to love anyone but you."

"No, you must. Please." Sarah coughed again and her hand moved and then stopped. After a while, she said, "It's all right. I'll be all right." Then she didn't say anything else.

The doctor came into the room and looked at Sarah and put his hand on Bill's shoulder. "You have to go. I'll call you if there's any change."

Bill stood outside Sarah's room with his forehead pressed hard against the cold wall. Soon they came for him but it was too late. Sarah had already gone far away and there was no way he could reach her or even think about her clearly.

He stood beside her bed and did not listen while the doctor explained what had happened. He stared at them and stared at them until the air filled with flames and they ran away. When they were gone, he crawled onto the bed beside Sarah. He kissed her mouth and ran his hands over her chest and down over her flattened stomach and between her legs. But it was like touching a statue.

He got up and walked out of the hospital, past Ira toward the train station, the bitter wind blowing his tears away.

III

The train swayed as it picked up speed and clacked southward. Bill lay on top of the boxcar until they crossed the American border.

Then he slid down between the cars out of the dry dusty wind. He stared vacantly at the bleak land that rolled past. Long empty miles of shifting plain and dying farms slipped past as the sun crawled its slow way across the sky. The sun was red through the hazy dust that filled the air. Bill stared at it until it burnt a red spot against his brain. Along one side of the red disk a thin black sliver was cut away. Bill watched as the sliver grew larger then receded until the red orb was whole once more. The black sliver inside of him continued to grow.

After a while clouds began to gather and finally a light welcome rain began to fall. Bill shivered and slowly moved along the side of the boxcar to an open door. He went through it into the cool dark interior.

There was a smell and a faint shuffling stir. He was not alone. A dirty man was sitting at one end of the car half buried in bits of old cloth and rubbish. He had long stringy brown hair that was matted around his head like a hood. His face was wide and heavily lined, except around his eyes which were remarkably smooth and clear like those of a young boy.

They watched each other for a long time. Finally the man at the end of the car spoke.

"I'm William. Who are you?"

Bill laughed.

"What's so funny, young fella?" William said angrily. Bill laughed again and told the old man his name. William laughed.

"We must be long lost brothers. Young Bill and old William. Senior and Junior. Have a drink." William thrust a dark green bottle toward Bill. Bill took a long swallow of wine. He pushed the bottle back and reached into his pocket and pulled out two apples. He threw one to William who caught it, rubbed it on his jacket and bit into it. The juice dribbled down his chin and William wiped it on his sleeve and looked down at the bottle.

They finished the bottle and when it was done William went to the open boxcar door and stood there staring out. After a moment he threw the bottle out the door and stared after it. He laughed and did a little dance. "Got him. Got him. Fucking railway cops." He went and sat back down in the pile of rags.

Bill watched William for a long time as the train rolled through Montana. At last he said, "You look like you've seen a lot more than I have."

William nodded. "Yup, it sure looks that way."

"What does it all mean? People are born, they live, they die and it doesn't seem to matter how good they are or how bad they are. It's all the same, except maybe the good die a little faster and a little more cruelly."

William looked up at the roof of the boxcar with his young old eyes. He stared up for a long time as if he could see something written there or maybe could see right through the dirty brown slats and on up to heaven. "I'll tell ya what it means," he said at last. "It don't mean shit."

FIVE

I

AMINESIS—THE DEATH OF MEMORY. AMINESIS—THE DEATH OF MEMORY. Aminesis—the death of memory. It is a code I decide. A fascist code.

There are straps across the bed so I can't move. Outside the window of my hospital room the sun is setting. I can't remember the last time I had a shit. I wonder if it is something to worry about.

I look at the calendar on the wall. It is an English calendar. That is a clever touch. These fascists are tricky. The calendar says it is 1999. December. All the days have been marked out with a felt pen except the last one. This is obviously meant to fuck me up. They must think I'm crazy. It is not 1999. Eleven years do not disappear without a trace.

I look over at the wall. There is a poster there. It says: "Aminesis—the death of memory." I have a feeling I've seen it before but I can't be sure. I decide it is some kind of fascist code. The sun is going down outside the window of what appears to be a hospital room and I wonder when they will undo these fucking straps so I can take a shit. I can't remember the last time I went to the bathroom and this worries me. Beside the poster on the wall is a calendar. It is an English calendar. Damn tricky, these fascists.

II

A swastika has been painted in bright dripping red across the wall near the side entrance to the new cathedral at Salamanca. Beneath it, a Spanish slogan calling for death to fascists has been scrawled in foot-high letters. Someone has tried to scrub the paint away but it has permanently stained the stone blocks. I rub my right fist and grin savagely in agreement.

I cross the sun-drenched plaza to the entrance and slip inside, through the brass-bound red doors. It is a relief to escape the sun and the ornate carvings that writhe up the outside of the Gothic structure. The church is nearly empty. The young never come here. The cathedral is left to the tourists and a few sad old women dressed in black. There is little room for Franco's church in modern socialist Spain.

I walk slowly toward the sanctuary. Two women sit in the front pew, praying silently over their rosaries. I look up the fluted columns that support the transept arch. Light flows from the windows at either end of the transept. Above the altar is a single window and above that three more in a row overlooking a high balcony. Light also streams down from the richly-carved cupola which has windows looking out on each of the major points of the compass.

I take the opera glasses out of my pocket and examine the walls and the roof of the cathedral. I pay particular attention to the ornate rings that circle the columns and the delicately carved ledges that run the length of the cathedral below the row of windows set high in the walls. Hidden among the larger carvings of angels and saints are scenes of bare-breasted nuns being chased by priapic bishops. One small picture almost hidden by the wings of a beatific angel at the base of the cupola shows a naked woman who has been caught by four of the grinning clergymen. They are merrily thrusting away in whatever orifice they can find. Wherever you go in Europe you can find these carvings in the old cathedrals, put there centuries ago by priest-hating masons. I wonder what the praying women might think if they knew.

At one side of the building is one of the largest pipe organs in Europe. It is seldom played now but must have been glorious in its day. It too is marked by the anti-clericism that one should expect from an old university town. The dark wood is so richly carved that it is easy for the eye to miss the occasional leering priest with his tongue hanging out as he stares at the bare breast of a sister. I manage to spot high up on one panel an erection sticking out from beneath a monk's robe.

I walk to the far side of the cathedral to a small wooden door. I step through it five hundred years farther into the past. Within the walls of the gothic New Cathedral lies a twelfth century romanesque one. It is small and low and dark compared to its enveloping successor. There is a greater sense of God here. I sit on the low simple benches and stare up at the intricately painted retable that stands behind the altar. In the apse of the church is a bright mural depicting the Judgement Day.

Christ, naked save for a cloth about his loins, stands astride clouds at the centre of the mural, his head surrounded by a golden aura and his right arm raised in anger. The stigmata show brightly on his hands and feet. He is surrounded by eight winged angels blowing trumpets or carrying spears. To one side kneels the Virgin Mary and, to the other, also kneeling, is a man dressed in a bearskin and crimson robe and carrying a miter, perhaps Joseph or a local saint. They are praying for the souls of the dead.

Beneath Christ and the angels are the resurrected dead. To the left, at Christ's right hand, are the saved, all in white robes and with hands and faces raised to heaven. On the other side are the damned. These poor folks are naked and are being driven into the mouth of a dragon who gapes wide to swallow them. In the mouth of the dragon are demons who seem to be helping it with its digestion. Some of the damned look up to Christ in fear, hope, or, simply confusion, but most are turned away, looking down. Between the two crowds are graves spewing up the dead. I note that only one of the graves is producing saints while nine of them are giving out crowds of sinners.

All in all, it is a very comforting sight. I look up at Christ's face with my binoculars. His long brown hair frames his face like a hood and his grey wide-set eyes seem to be looking right at me.

I ALWAYS LIKE GOING TO churches. You never know what you might find there. I found Sylvie in a church in Montreal and we've been together now for five years. It seems doubtful that we will be together much longer. I listen to the clicking of her heels on the cobblestones. It is an angry sound. We have been fighting almost continuously for a week, ever since we landed in Madrid. So much for the idea of a second honeymoon to revitalize our marriage. Sometimes I wonder what the point of all this is. Sometimes I feel like I am falling down a hole into a pit. The fire below is a tiny point of light and I am rushing headlong toward it. I am not in a good mood.

We leave the Plaza Mayor. Outside the House of Shells we are stopped by an older man in a dark suit. He has a handful of pamphlets printed in both English and Spanish. He presses one into my hand. I push it back at him.

"Que es?" Sylvie asks in her faltering Spanish.

"The truth about Guernica." He smiles and bows. "You must not believe the lies the communistas spread about the Phalanges. This tells what really happened. This is about the real Spain, not the lies of that bastard Gonzalez."

I have voted Tory all my life but in Spain I would support Gonzalez and the socialists. I spit on the ground in front of the man.

"Jew killer." I growl at him. "Chinganda Fascista. Baby burner. Rapist! Fucking piece of shit murderer."

The man blanches beneath his brown skin. He pushes me and snarls like a dog. I lash out with my right hand and catch him flush on the jaw. He sits down hard on the pavement. He drops his pamphlets and they begin to blow away in the wind. He is crying. I turn and walk away. Behind I hear the slap of his leather soles as he runs down the street and around the corner. Other tourists are staring at us and two young Spanish men are laughing. I keep walking.

Sylvie is furious. She grabs me by the shoulder and spins me around. Her face is bright red, as if it were on fire.

"How could you do that? He was a harmless old man."

"He was a Nazi."

"He was an old man, fighting for a lost cause."

"If you fight, you had better expect to get hurt." I turn and keep walking. Sylvie calls after me, her voice harsh with anger. "You are nothing but a bully. A cruel, insensitive, stupid bully."

"Hey," I say as I turn back. "I resent the part about being stupid." I laugh but Sylvie doesn't find it funny. She turns and stomps back toward the hotel. I watch her go. I still enjoy watching her walk in heels.

WHEN WE LAND AT THE airport in Madrid, a man with our name on a card meets us outside of customs. He walks us out of the terminal and across two parking lots to a small red car. He takes an impression of our credit card with a portable plate, the kind hookers use, and we sign the contract.

I look at the car with some concern. It is a standard. I have a lot of trouble with standards, so even though it is my turn to drive, I persuade Sylvie to do it for me while I navigate. She is a better driver than I am anyway, though I would never admit that to her.

It seems pretty straightforward. I had picked out an area of the city that had lots of little cheap *pensiones*. We would drive down there and park. Tomorrow or the next day we would take a side trip down to Toledo and then a few days after that we would go up to Salamanca and then on to Portugal.

There are nearly one million cars in Madrid but only sixty-eight thousand parking spaces downtown, most of them hidden where you can't find them. It seems on this particular day that most of the cars in Madrid are driving around the twenty or so blocks that make up the city centre looking for those last few parking spaces. Cars are parked everywhere, on sidewalks, on the meridians of streets, on any unoccupied piece of pavement or unfenced piece of grass.

It turns out that the area of the downtown that I choose as our base can only be reached by a single route. This is true of most places in Madrid, where almost every street is one-way, made worse by the large blocks that are completely closed to vehicular traffic.

The route that we are required to follow calls for a sharp right turn at a five-street intersection. When Sylvie approaches the intersection she refuses to make the turn because she says I am asking her to turn into a one-way street going the wrong way. She accuses me of trying to kill her.

After twenty minutes of driving in a huge circle we manage to return to the same intersection. Again Sylvie refuses to make the turn although I do point out to her the street we are turning into is a one-way street going the right way. She says I am lying. A pigeon circling the city overhead shits on our windshield. We decide to go to a different hotel.

Three hours later and we're still in the car. It is almost completely dark but traffic in the city hasn't abated. In fact it seems to be getting worse. At one point I look up at Sylvie and say, my voice shaking with horror and despair, "We've driven off the fucking map."

Sylvie pulls into a park by the side of the road. It is a big park but there is almost no one there. There are very few lights and the dark trees hang over the car. They seem to be watching us. We sit in the dark and stare at each other. Sylvie starts to cry. So do I. After a minute we both start to laugh.

We find a sign with the name of the park, Casa del Campo. I find it on the edge of the map and we head back into the city. I spot a hotel that has its own parking but we miss the turnoff. Sylvie pulls into the train station and waits while I go back and check in. She pulls back onto the road. Fifteen minutes later we are sitting back in front of the train station.

This is when I learn that no cab driver in Madrid speaks English. I walk up to the taxi stand at the train station while Sylvie sits in the car and waits. I plan to ask one of these old men to drive our car to the hotel. They do not understand. Of course they don't. It is a ridiculous request. The hotel is less than a hundred metres away. I find that it is impossible to find anything in my phrase book remotely related to getting someone to drive your car one hundred metres to a hotel.

I take out the hotel key and a thousand peseta bill, about five times the cost of a taxi ride across the city. I gesture toward the car where Sylvie is sitting, smiling at us. The men start to laugh and wink at each other. I suddenly realize what they must be thinking. I thank them and go back to the car.

We sit in the car at the train station until eleven o'clock when the traffic finally begins to clear. We drive out onto the street and make two quick illegal turns that bring us to the hotel. We park the car and leave it there until we leave Madrid for Salamanca four days later. We sit in our hotel room and drink wine and do not talk to each other until we are in the car leaving the city.

This is the beginning of the end.

III

I work my arms free of the straps and manage to release them. I sit up in the bed. I try to remember who strapped me down and why. There is a diary beside the bed and I look at it. The entries make no sense to me.

The last entry is the word, Dion. I wonder who Dion is.

I must have had an accident. Maybe the plane crashed in Madrid. I think this must be the case because I remember nothing of our trip to Spain. I wonder if Sylvie is okay.

There is a poster on the wall. Aminesis—the death of memory. I shake my head. The calendar beside the poster says 1999. Eleven years cannot disappear like that.

I get out of the bed and go to the bathroom. I want to piss but I can't and it worries me. I put my penis back in my pyjamas and turn to look in the mirror. I look old, just like my father before he died. There is a scar on my forehead. I want to scream but a voice in my head tells me not to. The voice says that I'll be all right. Everything will be all right. The voice tells me that I must prepare for a journey. It is the most important journey I will ever take. That anyone has ever taken.

I go back to the bed and lie down. I am not afraid anymore. I close my eyes and go to sleep.

I am dreaming. I am walking down the street but I am tired of walking. So I think for a minute and then I am floating a few inches above the ground. I skim along the ground faster and faster. I zip in and around people and buildings but no one seems to notice me. No one thinks it's odd that I am floating. I float up to one young man and stop. He has long hair. It is brown and shiny and frames his broad face like the cowl of a monk. He smiles and looks at me with wide-set grey eyes. "I am waiting for you," he says.

I wake up screaming.

SIX

I

AFTER SPENDING TWO WINTERS ON HIS BROTHER'S SHEEP RANCH IN Montana, William left and came south to Colorado, looking for work on the Great Water Diversion Project started by President Roosevelt. He and Harry, the eldest of the four Anderson brothers, had fought constantly, mostly about William's religion and Harry's drinking. William left when he couldn't stand it anymore.

The night before he left, William had a vision of his brother being dragged off to hell by an enormous lizard while a white-robed Jesus looked on with wide-set grey eyes. The flames of hell had licked up out of the ground and consumed Harry. In the morning William set fire to his brother's barn and left.

Harry managed to put the fire out before it caused too much damage. He thought of sending the state troopers after his brother but finally thought better of it and, instead, had a few drinks to toast William's departure.

In Colorado, William told people that he was from Maine so he wouldn't be deported and sent back to Canada. He knew that lying was a sin and spent many hard nights praying for forgiveness. At last, Jesus spoke to him and told him it was a necessary evil. There were many sinners in Colorado and William was charged with their redemption.

William found a place to stay on a farm not far from the dam site. There were two other men staying there, twin brothers from Utah.

The farmer's wife had died the year before and he had lost the heart to work his fields. Instead he took in lodgers and worried about his fifteen-year-old daughter.

William tried to convert the twins from Utah to his vision but they were caught in some strange religion of their own and only tried to convert him in return. The farmer and his daughter would sometimes pray with him but continued to go to their own church. William did not go to church, for his vision had told him that organized religion was sinful and filled with corrupt men. Instead he prayed in the barn or in clearings in the woods behind the farm. Later, much later, he built a rough stone chapel in the woods beside a stream.

The twins from Utah worked on the dam and they introduced him to the field boss who liked his strong clean looks and hired him on. William worked hard and never missed a day, no matter what the weather or circumstances. He tried to convert his fellow workers during the lunch breaks but this led to many fights and he was warned that he would lose his job if he didn't stop. William was silent for a long time after that, doing his job and ignoring the sinners around him. During this time he prayed for guidance and tried to think of another way to complete his mission.

One day a voice came to him and told him what to do. Soon he began to steal dynamite from the dam site.

II

William sat up in bed and looked around. The room was cool but his face glistened with sweat. His throat felt tight around the scream trapped inside.

It was early. The light of pre-dawn filtered through the thin cotton curtains that covered the window. In the bunk across the room he could hear the gentle snores of Abel and Ephraim Baker, the twins from Utah. Abel turned restlessly in his sleep and called out softly for his mother.

William lay back on the thin mattress of his cot and pulled the blanket up around his chin. He tried to go to sleep again but he couldn't. He had been dreaming.

In the dream, he had been fucking Alice, the young daughter of Jonathon Cobb, master of the decrepit farm where he and the Baker boys lived. He was doing it from behind, the way animals do it. He looked up and saw Sarah staring at him. She was holding their dead baby in her left arm while holding the hand of an enormous shadowy man dressed in black. There was a fire behind the man so that his frame was haloed in red light and William could not see his face. When he looked back down at Alice, he saw that her skin was shiny and scaly and was sloughing away from her like the skin of a snake. She looked back at him, her head twisted at an impossible angle and there were insects crawling out of her eyes.

William got up and put on his clothes. He crept down the back stairs and out through the kitchen. No one else was awake. He went into the yard and walked around to the barn. He went inside and took a set of reins down from their peg on the wall. He took one of the thin leather straps and snapped it between his hands, the crack echoing from the walls of the stable. A horse whinnied in surprise.

William knelt in the middle of the barn floor and unbuttoned his shirt. He took it off and carefully folded it and laid it on the floor in front of him. Gripping the strap firmly in his right hand, he tilted his head forward and began to whip the strap over his shoulder onto his back. As he did so he recited the Lord's Prayer.

> *Our Father who art in heaven (crack)*
> *Hallowed be Thy name (crack)*
> *Thy kingdom come (crack)*
> *Thy will be done (crack)*
> *On earth as it is in heaven (crack)*

When he had finished the prayer using his right hand he switched to his left and repeated it. As the last stinging blow landed, he fell forward onto the floor and lay there with his arms outstretched until he heard the household begin to stir to life. The blood had clotted and dried on his back so he took his shirt and carefully put it back on. He got up and went into the house.

Alice was in the kitchen making breakfast. When William came through the back door she was bending forward to put bread in the oven for supper, her round ass stuck high in the air. William stared at her and felt a stirring. He grabbed the front of his shirt and pulled the cloth tight against his back, gasping as the rough red wool rubbed across the raw welts that criss-crossed his flesh. All thoughts of Alice raced from his mind.

By the time breakfast was ready, the Baker twins had finished washing up and even old man Cobb was out of bed. Alice served each of them a big plate of scrambled eggs, thick slabs of bacon and heavily buttered slices of yesterday's bread. They washed it down with mugs of fresh milk. To finish it off, Alice doled out a single cup of honey-sweetened coffee to each of them.

William went out and sat on the back step and looked toward the woods and at the mountains that loomed in the distance. There was no work today as it was Sunday. Soon the Cobbs would head into town to go to church. The Baker twins would sit in the room they shared with William and read to each other all day. On Sundays, William could not go to his own room. William would take his rifle and go back in the woods to hunt rabbits or partridge or whatever the day offered. He would stop at his chapel and count the growing pile of dynamite that he stored there. When the time came he would use the dynamite to blow up the dam he was helping to build, bringing on a flood to cleanse the valley of sinners.

For now, he sat on the step and stared out at the mountains. He let his mind clear and waited for the voice to come and speak to him. This morning it did not come. William sighed and looked toward the stable. Perhaps, he thought, I am not yet pure. He forced himself to lean back against the rough wood of the door frame and let the clean waves of pain wash over him.

William was still sitting on the back step when he heard Cobb and his daughter get in their wagon for the short drive to church. He looked up into the sky to where a single black crow was flying in a steady circle round and round the farm yard. He got up and went into the house. He climbed the stairs to his room and got his rifle and a box of shells. Ephraim Baker looked up from his book and stared at William as he entered. William stared back and then turned on his heel and left.

When he went back outside, the crow was still circling overhead, so he shot it.

III

William finished skinning and gutting the last rabbit and laid its naked carcass alongside the other two on the kitchen table. He carefully wiped the blood off his knife and coated it in a thin layer of oil before sliding it back into its sheath. Each body was perfect and untouched. He had hit the heads cleanly with a single shot so that none of the meat was damaged. He scooped up the entrails and carried them outside for the dog. He stretched the three skins across the rack he had built for that purpose. He washed them with tea and put them out to dry in the sun. Later, he would make mittens for the winter.

He went back into the kitchen and picked up his rifle to clean it. He cracked it open to check that the chamber was clear and empty. As he did so, the front door opened and Jonathon and Alice Cobb came back from church. William snapped the rifle shut and leaned it against the kitchen table.

As he always did after church, Jonathon Cobb climbed the stairs to his room above the kitchen to read the Bible. Alice came into the kitchen and took the bread out of the oven and set it on racks beside the counter. She looked at the three rabbits on the counter, smiled at William, and put them in the ice box.

"I'll cook those tonight for supper if you like," Alice said. "I was going to kill a chicken but rabbit stew would be much nicer."

William nodded. "I was hoping you might say that."

William always liked this time after the Cobbs came home from church and was happy that he had managed to catch the rabbits so quickly. It was as if the animals had been told to wait for him at the edge of the woods.

Alice started to sing one of the hymns they had played during the service. William watched as she danced and twirled around the kitchen. Alice was always like this after church.

As William watched he thought again about the disturbing dream from the night before. He realized what it meant. Sarah had come to tell him that this was the girl he was supposed to be with. Sarah had died because of their sin of being together before they were married. Alice died and corrupted in his dream to tell him that. He would have to wed Alice before he slept with her.

Alice's skirt twirled and lifted as she danced so William could see her legs above the knees. He tore his gaze away. Alice went to the cupboard and bent over to take out a stewing pot for the rabbits. William found himself staring at her as she bent over. He turned away and looked down. He wiped a bit of spittle from the corner of his mouth.

Alice went out of the kitchen and came back carrying a large pail of water from the well. Some of the water had spilled from the bucket and splashed the front of her dress. Alice swore and picked up a cloth from the bench, wiping the water from her chest. Her breasts were pressed against the wet cloth and William could see her small nipples harden and rise.

William grabbed his gun and shoved a bit of wadding into the barrel. He picked up the long metal cleaning rod and shoved it down the barrel, hard. The rod came down on the bullet in the chamber with great force pushing it back against the firing pin. Alice walked across the kitchen toward the root cellar door. As she walked in front of the barrel of the gun, it went off.

The rod, followed by the bullet, flew out of the gun ripping the flesh of William's right hand as it went. It passed up through Alice's throat, cutting off the second verse of "Jesus Loves Me." It continued up through her mouth and into her brain and on through her skull, blowing a hole the size of a tea saucer in the top of her head. Bits of bright white bone and globs of blood and brain spattered across the kitchen. For a moment, the air was full of red flames and grey oily smoke.

The rod continued up through the ceiling into Jonathon Cobb's room. It passed three inches to the left of where the old man was sitting in the rocking chair reading from his Bible. He read as it passed through the air beside him: *My strength is dried up like a potsherd; and my tongue cleaveth to my jaws; and thou has brought me unto the dust of death.* The rod struck the ceiling of his room and embedded itself there, sending a shower of plaster down onto Cobb's head.

Cobb gave a gurgling cry and leapt to his feet. He stumbled from his room and down the stairs. The Baker twins came hard on his heels. When they burst into the kitchen, William was still sitting at the kitchen table, the rifle between his legs. He was holding his bloody hand in front of him and staring at it. He was covered in blood and brains and bone.

Alice lay on the kitchen floor in a spreading pool of crimson. Her face was unmarked and was turned toward her father as if in repose. Cobb walked across the floor and knelt in his daughter's blood. He scooped her up in his arms and squeezed her tight against his chest. He looked up at heaven and he howled.

William wiped his hand across his chest and across his stomach and shoved it between his legs. The gun was hard against his hand. He let it drop to the floor. He slowly got up and went to the door. He looked back at Cobb and his daughter and then over at Abel and Ephraim who stood pallid and shaking against one wall. Then he turned away and went through the door into the yard.

The sky was as black as night and streaked with fire. The dark man looked down on him and laughed.

William set off at a run across the empty fields and into the woods. He ran through narrow grassy trails until he came to the stone chapel by the stream. He gathered together the sticks of dynamite he had stored there.

Then he blew the chapel to smithereens.

SEVEN

I

I WAKE UP SCREAMING.

Usually when you dream you are barely asleep. You are drifting right below consciousness, on the very surface of sleep. This is called REM sleep. REM stands for rapid eye movement. As you dream your eyes move quickly from side to side under your eyelids, the same way they do when you are watching a movie.

Sometimes you dream when you are deep asleep. When this happens you do not move at all. You are dreaming in the deepest level of the unconscious where your most primitive anxieties and fears lurk, waiting for you. When you wake up with your heart pounding and your breath catching at the raw edges of your throat and with nothing in your mind but naked fear, you have been walking with the monsters.

I know that I have been deeply asleep because I cannot remember why I am afraid. I have been dreaming of monsters.

It is dark in the room. Outside the door, footsteps approach, stop and then recede.

I must be back in town at the hotel. I can't remember how I got here. I feel confused. The dream has disturbed me. I lie down and try to go back to sleep.

II

I feel like I am being watched. I look up the trail that leads back to the mouth of the fjord. It climbs the side of the long tongue of the gravel moraine that spills down from the glacier lip towards the river. No one is visible among the rocks. I look down along the line of gravel toward the water. The pass is at its narrowest point here and the Owl River, which has meandered peacefully for some kilometres down the broad valley, here deepens and races between the narrow cut between the huge piles of gravel and rock.

I turn and look back up the pass toward Summit Lake. I slip my pack off and lean it against a lone rock that sits on the edge of the long sandy flat. I sit on the rock and take a cigarette out of my vest pocket and light it. It is my last one. Quitting time. Again.

I draw the smoke into my lungs, hold it for a moment, savouring the slight rush, then exhale through my nose.

I came here to be alone, not to be watched. The side of the mountain opens up and a face peers down at me. The mountain closes again.

I take another drag from the cigarette, then carefully butt it out and put it back in the pack. I can quit later. The sand flat stretches away in the distance, beige under the bright northern sun. About three kilometres away it ends against the side of another rocky slope. Across the slope I can barely make out the grey-green vegetation that clings to the rocks and gravel.

Thor dominates the horizon the same way the thunder god dominated Asgard. The face of the mountain towers over the valley, the top of it leaning out at a ten-degree angle. Now it lies in shadow, its features dark and obscured. Later the sun will shine across it and I will be able to see the long purple ledge that runs diagonally across the plane of the mountain like a scar. Two years ago, a team of Japanese climbers was returning from scaling the higher mountains further inland. The leader of the camp couldn't sleep so he decided to try a midnight ascent. He slipped out of camp and began his solo climb. About thirty metres from the top he forgot to secure his piton before reaching for a jutting point of rock above his head. The rock crumbled in his hand and he fell nearly a kilometre. Because he forgot to check.

Aminesis—the death of memory.

I take out my binoculars and look back along the trail. At the top of the far hill I can see a group of three hikers. Their bright blue and red windbreakers stand out sharply against the earthy tones of the hill. I remember these three from the camp at Summit Lake. They had carted in complete sets of pots and pans and loads of fresh meat and vegetables. Their packs must have weighed over sixty pounds. Thirty kilograms. I make a note to myself to stop thinking in imperial measures. It is hard.

I pick up my pack and slip it back onto my throbbing shoulders. I turn away from Thor and start off, my head bent forward as I stare at my boots. I only stop for rests when I get tired of looking at my boots and need a reminder of why I came here.

I am almost at the top of the hill when I get a sharp twinge in my lower back. I straighten up in pain and, when I do, I lose my balance. My pack pulls me backward and I fall back and slide down the hill until I come up hard against a rock. There is a flash of fire across my eyes and then blackness. When I open my eyes there is a young man staring down at me with wide-set grey eyes. I blink and the face twists until it is not a young man at all. It is one of the hikers from Summit Lake. "Are you all right?" she asks.

I HAVE BEEN SITTING AT Summit Lake in the rain for nearly three days. It is getting crowded here and each day I move my tent a little further north. It is useless. There are now six tents crowded along the west side of the long lake. Unless I move down into the wild country I am stuck with these visitors. The weather is miserable and I have no desire to wade through a waist-deep glacial stream simply to get a little bit of privacy. I crawl into my tent and close the flaps. When people walk by, I pretend I am not there.

On the morning of August 1st, I crawl out of my tent and look up into the heavens. It is snowing. From deep inside me wells a powerful emotion. Words come bursting through my brain and out my mouth. "What the fuck am I doing here?" I pack up my gear and head back towards the mouth of the fjord.

By noon, there is a wind howling down out of the pass hard enough to move small stones across the ground. This is good, for several reasons. First, the wind is at my back and will make walking easier, unless, of course, it blows me off a rock and into the river. Second, it will keep most people in their tents. It will certainly keep boats out of the fjord. I will have the trails entirely to myself. I should not meet anyone coming up the pass until long after the wind has died. Finally, and most importantly, I simply love the wind.

As I walk along, I have to be careful that I do not lean too far forward. If the wind catches my pack it could flatten me. I stop after a bit and look up at one of the waterfalls that tumbles down the sides of the sheer cliffs from its glacial source. The wind is blowing it back up the side of the mountain until it disappears in a cloud of mist.

I am twenty-seven years old. I have spent my life savings to come here. I am cold and I am sore. I look around at the low scudding clouds and whirling snowflakes. The wind is cutting and almost knocks me over. I shift the heavy pack on my shoulders trying to find a patch of muscle that isn't bruised and aching. I wonder why I am here.

The ground opens up in front of me. A tall gangly man climbs up out of the hole and smiles at me. He reaches out his hand and grasps my shoulder. He points up the side of the mountain to a doorway. Light is pouring through the doorway. It is very bright and inviting. I shake his hand off my shoulder and turn away. When I turn back both he and the doorway are gone.

I realize that I have no answer to my mainly rhetorical question. I adjust my pack and continue walking down the trail. I think about it some more.

The simple answer is that I am trying to understand the point of it all. I suppose, to be honest, I am trying to cope with my father's death. He turned forty-five last September and four days later dropped dead from a heart attack. It's very unnerving to have your father die that young. I stop and look around. There is no one in sight. I continue on down the trail.

I don't know what the more complex answer is. Perhaps, I would like to believe in some greater cosmic purpose—God, if you like. This seems unlikely but I think about it seriously for a while.

I hear a seagull. I look up and see that three of the grey-white birds are flying overhead in wide circles. I am amazed that they can stay aloft in this wind but they do. I take some cereal from my pack and throw it into the air. The wind catches it and carries it high. The seagulls dart after it but I can't tell if they get any or not.

By supper, I am too tired to walk anymore. I throw my pack down and pitch my tent between two large rocks. The wind has died a little but I still need to weigh down the corners with hunks of stone to keep it from blowing down the pass to the sea. I make a quick supper from my store of freeze-dried food and crawl into the tent for the night.

I lie beside the young man with the long brown hair. His body feels nice against mine and, on an impulse, I run my tongue across his chest and down over his taut belly. His cock is hard and I let him come in my mouth. We talk for a while about nothing of consequence. He tells me the world will end in the morning. We roll over so our backs are pressed together and fall asleep.

In the morning, the wind has completely died away and it is a beautiful sunny day. I get up and pack my gear. I start down the trail. I am making good time and should reach the mouth of the fjord by tomorrow. It is easier now that I don't have to walk and can float above the ground.

I am watching myself float and realize that I am lying in a bed with straps across my chest watching myself watch myself float. I am standing beside the bed watching myself lying in the bed watching myself watch myself float. And so on. At the time it doesn't seem important but, later, I think it is.

I cross a stream that runs across a rocky slope above a long flat sand bank. It is early morning and the stream is still very low. I step from rock to rock, careful not to let my pack pull me over. When I was walking up to Summit Lake I crossed this stream in the afternoon and it was knee-deep. The water comes directly from a glacier tongue across his chest and is very cold. My legs go numb in seconds when I step into it.

I walk down the slope until I reach the broad beige-coloured sand flat. In the distance I see a solitary hiker sitting on a rock. He is looking at me through a pair of binoculars. As he sees me, he gets up and puts his pack back on. He climbs up the steep gravel moraine where the valley narrows. He is almost to the top when he suddenly falls backward and is lost to view among the rocks. I decide that this in no way affects me and I continue walking at the same steady pace.

For a while, a man that looks a lot like my father, except that he has a limp and a scar across his forehead, walks along beside me. He keeps stopping along the trail to pee but nothing comes. He looks quite funny, standing there in his pyjamas holding his penis in his hand so expectantly. I suppose one can get used to anything.

I reach a solitary rock on the edge of the sand bank. I slip my pack off and sit down looking back the way I came. Of course, I can see a lone hiker on the far side of the sand bank. I take out my binoculars to look at him but he is no longer visible. These appearances and disappearances are getting quite annoying. Somehow I don't remember it being quite like this.

THE BOAT DROPS ME AT the mouth of the fjord and I start off toward Summit Lake. The pilot of the boat, a tall gangly young man with enormous hands and wide-set grey eyes, follows me up the trail but I tell him to piss off and he does. The weather is pretty nice for Baffin Island in late July and I am pleased that I came. After an hour or so I get tired of walking and decide to float up to Summit Lake a few inches off the ground. This is tricky in places, especially on the loose gravel moraines and glacial streams. Despite these difficulties I reach Summit Lake in less than an hour and set up camp. There are hundreds of people here and it really is getting unreasonably crowded for a remote national park. I wonder what my tax dollars are being spent on if not for isolation. Of course, once I realize that almost all the people here are either me or the graceful young man with the burning hair, I don't feel so bad and tear up the sarcastic letter I was writing to my Member of Parliament.

After four days, I see God and leave.

III

There are all these men standing around my hospital bed with their penises in their hands trying to pee. You call it a penis when you are talking about urination and a cock when you are talking about fucking. This is the only way you can accept that you use the same thing to excrete waste and make babies. There may be an insight here about the great circle of life but it slips away before I can fully grasp it.

"Stop it!" I scream and the men go away and I am alone once more. I am sure I can figure this out if I can only remember where I am and why I am here.

This poster is a clue. Of that I am sure. Aminesis—the death of memory.

I get out of bed and go to the window. As I suspected I am in a hospital but I don't know where. I go into the bathroom and look at the lined face in the mirror. I wonder if I am actually my father.

I go back to the window and look out. There are lots of people coming and going so it is not too late. Not yet.

I look at the calendar on the wall. If it is to be believed, tomorrow is the first of January, the year 2000. I wonder where the last eighteen years have gotten to. Time flies.

A young man in a doctor's white coat comes into my room and asks me how I am feeling. I shrug my shoulders and he nods knowingly and goes out the window. I watch as he sails away towards the moonlight. The last I see of him he is walking up a fiery moonbeam into the night.

EIGHT

I

WILLIAM SLIPPED THE TINY PACK FROM HIS SHOULDERS AND PUT IT BESIDE the mossy log. He could hear the faint roar of the falls through the trees and he walked slowly in the direction of the sound. He liked the sound. He liked any sound that was not a human voice.

The forest floor was damp and soft. There was little growth in the smothering perpetual darkness beneath the green canopy of the trees. William reached out his hand and placed it on the cool rough bark of a tree. The trunk of the tree rose straight and unbroken until it reached the verdant arch of the forest roof. Here and there a bit of light trickled brightly through small gaps in the leaves and branches above, tiny windows on heaven.

William leaned against the trunk. He cried. The tears streamed down his face, his mouth open. No sound came from his open mouth. There was only the faint roar of the river and the steady drip of water from the trees.

William wiped his face and walked towards the river. The forest ended on the bank of a steep ravine. The sides of the ravine were clogged with thick new growth, vines and bushes struggling for survival in the bright sunshine. A hundred feet below, the river tumbled and foamed over a small waterfall, then widened into a smooth blue highway to the sea.

William looked across the ravine at the broad unbroken stretch of forest, thick tall trunks stretching away into the distance. He nodded with approval and walked back to the fallen log and sat down. He opened his pack and took out a piece of dried meat, wrapped in cloth. He unwrapped it and bit off a smoky mouthful and chewed it slowly. In the back of his head he could hear a small slippery voice begin to talk so he chewed harder and listened to the sound of his jaws working until the voice gave up and went away.

He took a long drink from his canteen, cool water sweetened with honey to give him strength. He thought briefly of his sister and of fire. He shook his head and took another drink.

He looked up once more into the high forest. It seemed like something was waiting to happen. He sat for a long time but nothing did. After a while, he got up and walked back the way he had come.

II

The barge made its slow way up the river until it reached the small waterfall. The captain steered it toward a small sandbar that lay on the right-hand side and the men jumped off and waded through the cold water up onto the sand. They pulled the barge up onto the soft ledge with thick corded ropes that they then used to secure it to the small trees that grew by the water's edge.

William stood on the front of the barge and pointed up the side of the ravine to the best place to set up camp. The foreman grunted his agreement and set the men to dragging their gear up the side of the steep hill.

By mid-afternoon the barge was unloaded, and, lightened of its load, could be floated off the sand bar. The captain waved farewell and steered the flat-bottomed boat back down the river to the sea. There it would hug the shore until it reached the new mill town thirty miles down the coast.

William sat on the mossy log and watched while the men expanded the small clearing to make a campsite. The ancient hoary trees shuddered and fell under the whining buzz of their saws. He smiled as he watched. He had led them to paradise and now he watched while they destroyed it. There is nothing wrought by God, he thought, that I cannot destroy.

In a few days he would depart to find a new part of Eden. For now, he was satisfied to sit and watch while the men cleared the camp and set up their tents. In the next few weeks, he knew, they would cut the fallen trees into rough planks and build shelters to carry them through the winter. By spring, every tree for as far as the eye could see would be flattened and cut into logs. When the ice was out of the river, they would roll the logs down into the swollen waters and float them in a huge mass down to the sea. On the edge of the sea they would be circled by a long boom made out of logs and chain and dragged down to the great mill town to be made into paper. Some of the paper would be used to print Bibles. William laughed.

After a bit, he tired of watching the big burly men scurry around like ants on a carcass. He got up and walked to the edge of the wood and looked off toward the still untouched trees. He walked slowly away from the camp until the sound of their shouting and the whine of the saws faded in the distance. His soft boots made hardly a whisper on the thick brown forest floor. He walked in a straight line away from the camp and the river until even the roar of the falls could not be heard and the only sounds were the faint susurration of the wind in the trees and his breathing. As he walked he noted each fallen log, each special signpost that had been established for his own particular guidance.

For the first time in a long time he let the voice talk in his head but he did not listen to it. He walked on through the forest so quietly that after a while it seemed like he was floating silently a few inches above the forest floor. He came across a young deer among the trees. He approached it where it stood motionless watching him. He put out his right hand, the fingers stiff and bent. At the last moment, the deer tossed its head and shied away from his hand, running off through the trees. William watched it until it disappeared in the distance.

William squatted down in a patch of ferns beside a tiny trickling stream. He dabbled his fingers in the cool water and traced a pattern in the dark algae-stained mud of the stream bed. He watched as the water washed away the pattern he had made. He carved another pattern, deeper this time, cutting into the mud with his fingers. Traces of his marks took longer to fade but the water kept flowing over them until they were gone. He scooped up mud from the bottom of the stream and made a small dam. At first the water pooled and slipped around and over the side of the dam cutting a new stream in the forest floor. William grinned. Then bit by bit the dam wore away until the stream returned to its original course. Only a trace of dirt and a small puddle of water marked the diversion he had created. As he watched, the pool of water sank into the ground and was gone.

William stood up, his knees cracking and twingeing. He walked over to a large boled tree and stood with his back against it. He pressed his head back against the bark and stretched his arms up and out to the sides. He waited.

After a while, the dark man walked through the forest and stood in front of William. He put his hand on William's chest and slid it down over his stomach to his crotch. He fumbled with the front of his pants and took out William's flaccid cock. William stood and stared at the man as he rubbed and squeezed. After a bit, the dark man gave up and walked away.

William stood with his back against the tree and his arms outstretched and waited. The September air was cool against his thighs but he made no effort to fasten his pants. Sarah walked out of the forest carrying their baby. She walked up to William and kissed him on the lips. Then she knelt down and took him in her mouth. William looked straight ahead into the forest. Her mouth was warm on his cock but he felt nothing else and after a while Sarah gave up and walked away.

William stood there for a long time waiting for whomever else might come, but no one did. As the sun began to set, he stepped away from the tree and did up his pants. He felt good. He listened but there was no voice in his head. He walked back through the forest to the camp.

III

In the morning, William crawled out of his tent and stretched. He had set up camp on the edge of the expanded clearing well away from the big canvas tents that served as temporary bunkhouses. The cooks were already up making breakfast. The smell of food wafted through the trees. William walked back into the forest and relieved himself.

He walked down to the river and stripped off his clothes. He dived into the clean cold water and swam out into the middle of the stream. He plunged down toward the river bottom, counting in his head as he did. One, two . . . fourteen, fifteen, until his lungs were aching. At last he reached the bottom . . . twenty, twenty-one. He scooped up a handful of stones and shot back to the surface . . . twenty-five, twenty-six . . . until he burst through it, his body rising until it was halfway out of the water, his lungs grabbing at air as he fell back into the river. He turned on his back and floated, kicking lightly for the shore. He looked at the stones clutched in his right hand. There were half a dozen small dark pebbles, a piece of rough red feldspar and a single white jag of quartz. He held the quartz up to the sun and could see a faint glint of yellow running in a vein along the stone. He felt a sudden fear for the river and let the stones fall from his hand back to the safety of the deep water.

William swam back to shore and rolled over and over in the thick ferns to dry himself. He pulled his clothes over his still damp body and walked back up the hill to the camp.

Everyone else was up. The last few men were stumbling from the tents, rubbing the sleep from their eyes. William got his mess and went over to the rough kitchen. The cook served him a big plate of scrambled eggs, thick slabs of bacon and heavily buttered slices of warm bread. William did not let it bother him. He poured himself a large mug of steaming coffee and went outside to eat.

He did not want to talk to anyone. He thought again about the dark man. He seemed very small now. The voice was only a faint tinny whisper. He thought of Sarah and Alice. He thought he might write to Jonathon Cobb. He looked down at the coffee.

William finished eating, wiping up the last of the egg and the bacon fat with a bread crust and popping it into his mouth. He wiped his mouth on his sleeve and poured the last of the coffee onto the forest floor. He took the dishes back into the kitchen and washed them. He went back to his tent and put the dishes away in his pack. He lay down on his bedroll and closed his eyes.

Our Father who art in heaven
Hallowed be Thy name . . .

It felt good to say the prayer in the old familiar way, the way he had learned as a very young boy on his father's farm. When he had finished, he said it again. He took a long breath and when he exhaled even the whisper was gone.

Outside he could hear shouting. He got up and crawled out into the air. The men were running towards the big central tent where the foreman had his office. William walked over to where they were gathered around the entrance of the tent. The foreman had hauled the radio out of the tent and set it on the flat stump of a tree. One of the men was turning the crank of the generator while the foreman talked into the heavy microphone. William could see the bright glow of the tubes through the back of the radio. The bright filaments danced like flames.

"When did it happen?" the foreman was shouting, as if somehow that would carry the message farther and faster through the air. "Say again. Over."

The speaker crackled and hissed. William could barely make out the words from the other end.

"Yesterday. The Brits declared a couple of days ago and

Parliament met yesterday. We're at war. Over."

The circle of men let out a whoop. William turned away. The voice came gibbering back into his head. William looked down and walked away. He screamed silently at the voice to shut up. He packed up his tent and put his pack on his back.

He went to the foreman and collected his pay. As he turned to go, the man put his hand on his shoulder and asked, "Where are you going now, Anderson?"

William shook his head and thought of bombed out churches in Europe. He could see birds flying through their split open naves. He shook his head and said over his shoulder, "Home. I'm going home."

NINE

I

It is getting very crowded in this room. Several of the men are standing beside the bed and studying the poster on the wall. Aminesis—the death of and so on. One of them is flipping through the calendar trying to find a date we can recognize.

I get up and walk to the window trailed by a line of younger and younger men. At the end of the line is a boy. I look at him. He should not be here yet. He turns away from my gaze and hangs his head. I look out the window and when I look back he is gone. The parking lot is nearly empty but there is still plenty of traffic on the road that runs by this building.

I go into the bathroom but there is an old man there peeing and several more are standing around with their penises in their hands, waiting. I give up and go back to bed.

I look down at my hands. My right hand is scarred. I clench it into a fist. I feel like a young man. There isn't one around so I sit on the bed with my eyes closed and listen to the murmur of confused voices in my head.

II

I am sitting on the top of a craggy hill looking down into a broad green valley. At the bottom of the valley is a stream. There is a cluster of stone buildings around an old water mill. I can see the wheel slowly turning in the water and see people moving around between the buildings. It is very pretty.

Monica is making tea over the campfire. Her cheeks are bright and her eyes sparkle as she smiles at me. I smile back and watch her make the tea. She is the most beautiful girl I have ever seen. She is certainly the most beautiful girl I have ever slept with. In fact, she is the only girl I have ever slept with.

I fly in a circle above the mountain top and look down on myself and Monica making tea. There is a flock of us up here and we fly in ever-widening circles over the Welsh countryside. Above is a flock of young men with long brown hair and wide-set grey eyes.

Monica and I drink the tea, hot and steaming and sweetened with honey. She thinks my name is David because that is what I have told her. I watch her and we talk about what's going on back home. I ask her if she thinks Nixon will resign and we wonder what ever happened to Trudeaumania. The whole time we are talking, all I think about is what she looks like with her clothes off.

After a while we stop talking and sit staring out across the grey and green countryside. On all the hills we can see flocks of sheep and young white lambs shining in the spring sun. To the north there is a lake, blue-grey in the distance and I imagine I can see a sailboat gliding across it.

A little later we go back into the tent and make love again. I let her get on top. I like the feel of the uneven ground beneath my back and I like to look up at her round breasts hanging down toward my face. I think it would be nice if she got pregnant, although she told me she's on the pill. I think it would be nice to father a child. After, we fall asleep. I wake up because I am cold and pull the blankets up around us. I run my tongue across Monica's breast and across her flat stomach and taste myself, sticky between her thighs. Then I pull her close to me and fall asleep.

I am dreaming. I dream that I am awake and flying in a circle overhead. I look down on the tent sitting on the crest of the hill. The red sun is going down and the tent looks like it's on fire.

WE GET OUT OF THE back of the truck and thank the farmer for the lift. The old truck sputters and coughs its way down the narrow gravel road and disappears behind a hill. I take Monica's hand and we walk along the narrow dirt trail that leads up the hill. When we are out of sight of the road, we stop and kiss for a while and then we continue up the hill between the low stone fences that mark the edge of the path.

We had come down from London on a lark. I met Monica at my friend's flat. It was a place he was squatting in, along a row of abandoned council houses, not far from the main campus of the University of London. I met Peter at a party in Toronto when he was back home for a visit and he told me to stop there if I ever came to London.

When I arrived, there were about a dozen people staying in the flat, stretched out on the floor or sharing the two beds that filled one room. Monica was there and a bunch of other people from Canada. There was a black guy from Jamaica and two girls from France.

Peter shared the place with a Welshman called Llewelyn, who didn't care how many people stayed there as long as they stayed out of his corner of the flat. Peter worked most days in a photo shop while Llewelyn did demolition work. He told me that this was the best job one could have since all you had to do was tear things apart and, because of the union, it was one of the best paid jobs in London. He made nearly forty pounds a week and, since he could live on less than ten, he was able to send a lot of money back to Wales to help his family.

One day Llewelyn came home from work all excited. He had a calendar he found when he was tearing down a house in North London. The calendar was from 1955 and showed a young boy and a girl tending a small flock of sheep on the crest of a rocky hill. Below, in the valley, you could see a stream with an old water mill on its banks, surrounded by a cluster of stone houses.

"I know these kids," Llewelyn said, his voice heavy with home. "I grew up with them. That's my home town right there." He pointed to the cluster of houses. "This one, right here, is where I was born."

"It must have changed a lot since then," I said. "It's been nearly twenty years."

"Ah, no," he replied. "Nothing has changed there in nearly two hundred years. I don't think it ever will."

I looked at the calendar. The boy in the picture looked back at me with wide-set grey eyes. I was born in 1955. I felt drawn to the picture. It was like falling down a well towards a shimmering pool of water, toward a single point of light at the far end.

Monica and I walk up the side of the hill toward the valley. Monica puts her hand on my shoulder. "I love you, David," she says. I kiss her on the mouth and turn away.

I GET OFF THE subway and ride the elevator to the surface. I look at the map that Peter gave me in Toronto. I check the address again and walk down the street. I am near the university and a lot of the people on the street are obviously students. Most of the men have long hair and everyone is dressed in bright colours. My own hair is short and my clothes are drab. People look at me as I pass.

I begin to grow nervous. I feel I am being watched. I look up suddenly and catch sight of a pigeon out of the corner of my eye. For a moment I thought I saw a man flying in a circle above my head but it is only this bird. I shake my head and laugh. The pigeon shits on the sidewalk in front of me.

I laugh as I fly over my head in London. I shit but miss the target by a few feet.

I finally get to Peter's place. It is getting dark and there are no lights from the windows of the row of houses except for a few guttering candles. There is neither electricity nor water in these houses. Peter warned me about that before I came. I go up to the door and knock. It is answered by the most beautiful woman I have ever seen. I introduce myself as David. Peter comes up behind her and stares at me, shrugs and doesn't say anything. I go inside.

III

These men are starting to annoy me. They are walking around, transparent as the skin of a snake. Some of them are laughing and seem happy. Most of them are not. I wonder what the connection between them is.

I think it has something to do with the calendar. Or maybe the poster. Or maybe the diary that lies open on the bed.

I get up. I notice I am limping. I think this is odd but some of the men are limping too, though most of them are not. A few of the men have erections and they seem very proud of this. Most of them are simply holding their penises in their hands, waiting to pee. The bathroom is always occupied.

I go to the window. It is the same old window. I stop for a minute, surprised that I recognize it. The feeling fades and I look out. On the horizon there is a bright light, getting closer. I cannot quite make it out yet. There is a dark man silhouetted in the light.

TEN

I

BILL GOT UP FROM WHERE HE WAS SITTING AND CROSSED THE MUDDY road. He nudged Allen awake with his boot. Allen stood up and stretched. A jeep came over the hill and drove by. The officer in the back looked at them as he passed. They saluted and he sketched the air in response. The jeep disappeared around a bend in the road and Allen squatted down beside the ditch.

"Fuck." The blond young man spat into the water that ran through the ditch. "I'll tell you, Pops. I'll be glad when this fucking war is over. I can hardly wait. There won't be no motherfuckers telling me what to do or when to do it. I'll sleep whenever I fucking well please and not to some fucking army schedule."

"There's always someone to tell you what to do, Allen," Bill sighed. "There always has been and there always will be."

"Hey, I thought we was fighting for fucking democracy." Allen laughed. "Isn't that right? I thought in a democracy no one could fucking tell you what to do. Fucking army."

Bill took a pack of cigarettes out of his shirt pocket and offered one to Allen. They lit up and sat on the muddy road while the smoke wreathed their faces and blew away in the wind.

Bill got up and started to walk down the road. "Don't fall asleep again, Allen. You're supposed to be on watch."

"Yes, sir." Allen flashed Bill a sardonic salute and slouched back on the ground. Bill pointed to the stripes on his arm. "Yes, sergeant."

Allen corrected. "Yes, Sergeant Pops."

Bill laughed and walked away. He was a lousy sergeant. Everyone thought of him as their older brother. The hard young men did better than the old regular army veterans. Bill shrugged. It didn't matter.

He just hoped he got through this all right. He wanted to go back to England. He wanted to lie with Violet, watch the baby grow inside her. He swallowed the lump in his throat. Since he had married Violet in the old country church outside London, he could think again about the future. He could pray to God again and go to church. He went to church with her every Sunday and, since coming to Europe, he went to chapel every Sunday. He never saw the dark man anymore except, sometimes, standing behind the enemy when he shot at them in the hills. He hardly ever heard the voice whispering to him, except late at night when he was lying in the hole he had dug for himself, listening to the shells whistling overhead and thinking about dying. Then, sometimes, the voice would come to him very quietly and softly and tell him that he wasn't going to die just yet, that he still had a long journey in front of him.

Bill finished the cigarette and threw the butt into the ditch. He walked down the muddy road and looked at the men sleeping in holes on either side of the road. They were all sleeping peacefully. Bill smiled.

"Hey, Pops. Checking in on the kids?" One of the men called to him.

"Go back to sleep, Davis. You'll wake the baby," Bill said softly. He kept walking down the line, until he reached the end. He sat down beside the sentry.

"Hi, Brownie. How's it going?" he asked.

Brownie passed him his tin cup and Bill took a sip of the steaming sweet coffee. "Hi, Bill." Brownie was only a few years younger than Bill and never called him 'Pops'. Brownie had introduced him to Violet at a YMCA dance and Bill knew he would think of him as a friend for a long time.

II

The orders came through that morning that they were to start the push towards Germany. Heavy fighting was expected but they were to move ahead as far as they could so as to force the enemy to solidify their lines. The British would bomb the German positions through the night and then the big American bombers would come in the morning to finish the job.

Bill got his platoon organized and informed the lieutenant when everything was ready. Lieutenant McIsaac was new to the platoon and didn't know many of the men's names yet. Bill walked beside him during the inspection. A little past ten they finally got moving.

Their company was to take a side road that swung up into the hills and ran parallel to the main road. Bill's platoon had the most experienced men and was sent to the vanguard. They moved along the narrow gravel road taking advantage of what cover they could find in the low scrubby trees that lined either side.

The land here was deserted. The stone fences between the overgrown fields were broken in many places. On the side of a hill a shattered farm house sat. One wall and part of the roof had collapsed. Bill sent Brownie and Davis to check for snipers but it was clean.

A little past noon, Bill called a halt. He looked back at the men gathered behind him. They were relaxed but alert. They laughed and talked among themselves while scanning the country ahead with wary animal eyes. Ahead, a few crows were circling slowly over the road.

Bill signalled to the others to stay behind while he and Allen slipped quietly along the side of the road. Bill pulled back the bolt of his sub-machine gun and cradled it lightly in his left arm, his right hand hovering near the trigger.

He almost stumbled over the man in the ditch before he saw him. He was young and blond. He wore the uniform of a lieutenant in the German army. His throat had been cut, his head was tilted at an impossible angle away from the gash so Bill could see the arteries and open windpipe in his neck. He gestured to Allen to be careful.

A few feet farther on there was an older man in a captain's uniform, his stubbly grey hair stained with blood where someone had bashed in the side of his head with the butt of a gun. Bill turned him over. He had a knife wound in his chest and another in his hip—a thin blade protruded from where it had broken off against the bone. His pistol was still strapped to his side, a 9mm Luger. Bill took it out of its holster and shoved it in the pocket of his coat. Beyond the captain was a sergeant, young like the lieutenant, and also stabbed to death and shoved into the bushes to hide him. There was a rifle beside him.

Bill squatted beside the bodies and wondered what they meant. Two officers and a non-com but no privates. All three had been killed from close up and the killers didn't even bother to take their weapons. That ruled out partisans. There weren't supposed to be any operating in this area anyway.

Bill sent Allen back to bring up the other men while he moved slowly on down the road. He stopped and looked to his left. He thought he had seen a man standing there watching him but there was no one there. He still had the feeling he was being watched. The space between his shoulder blades twitched.

Around a curve in the road were the remains of a camp. Clothing and other bits of gear, including some weapons, were scattered about. The tracks of several vehicles disappeared down the road while a mass of boot prints went up the side of the hill to the left.

Bill waited for the other men. He walked over to the lieutenant to see if he had any orders. The boy was sitting with his head in his hands. He looked sick. Bill nodded to Baker to stay with the officer while he led the men in a fan-shaped formation up the side of the hill.

The tracks led to the top of the hill and down into a little ravine on the other side. At the end of the ravine was the dark opening of a cave. The tracks disappeared on the stoney ground in front of the cave. Bill looked around but saw nothing. He sent men around either end of the ravine until he was sure that none of the enemy were lurking in the rocks of the surrounding hills. He dug into his shirt and pulled out the little phrase book they had issued him when they gave him his stripes.

He stumbled over the unfamiliar words: *"Ich bin ein soldat kanadischen. Ubergebe! Sie sind mein Gefangener."* There was no response. Bill fired a burst at the top of the cave. The bullets whined in the silence and a shower of sparks and stone chips fell over the opening.

There was a shout from inside the cave and then a white cloth was stuck out at the end of a long stick. Soldiers, boys really, not many of them over sixteen, stumbled out into the light, blinking like owls, with their hands held high above their heads. The few still carrying rifles threw them down on the ground as they emerged. The ravine filled up and the boys looked up at their captors, fear and hope mixed on their sunken faces. There were nearly ninety of them. Bill sent two men into the cave but it was empty. There were no officers or non-coms to be seen.

Bill marched his prisoners down the hill. He suggested that the lieutenant take charge and march the Germans back to the rear. McIsaac gratefully agreed and, taking two men, left Bill in command of the platoon. Bill felt relieved to be shed of the responsibility of looking after McIsaac.

The rest of the day was much the same and the company made rapid progress. Before supper they crossed the border and were well inside German territory when they halted for the night at the top of a low ridge, where the enemy line originally was. They had now pulled back to the next line of hills. The commander radioed their position back to headquarters so the bombers could establish new targets. As a reward for capturing the boys' brigade, Bill's platoon was assigned guard duty at the front of the ridge facing the enemy.

III

All night long the British bombed the shit out of the German line. It was quite a show. The entire ridge of hills was ablaze, long gouts of flame chasing clouds of black oily smoke into the sky. Bill slept while he could until Allen roused him for his turn at the front.

They had some trouble from German artillery but after a while the British bombers managed to pretty well knock it out so only the occasional shell whistled overhead. None of them landed near Bill and his platoon.

Around dawn, there was a brief respite. The British bombers headed back to base. Bill took out his binoculars and looked at the German line. Some of the enemy soldiers were crawling out of their foxholes and bunkers and were shaking futile fists at the departing Brits. It looked like there were plenty left to put up a fight when the company moved forward.

Not long after, Brownie came to relieve him. Bill walked down the ridge toward the mess tent. Most of the men had already eaten and were moving up to the top of the ridge to get ready to move out. Overhead, Bill could hear the drone of engines and looked up to see the flight of American bombers high overhead. He looked back up the ridge where most of the company was standing in the open. Some of them were looking up at the American planes and waving.

As the Americans came up over the ridge, Bill could see the bomb bay doors open. He watched the black specks grow larger and larger and then the top of the ridge exploded in flame. Bodies were flying everywhere, bodies and trees and bits of rock. A soldier halfway up the hill dived under a truck for cover just as it was hit by a friendly American bomb and burst into flame. Bill could hear him screaming under the wreckage.

Bill ran up the hill. Then he was floating a few inches above the ground and skating over the broken dirt and bodies, skating through the flames and oily smoke. He stopped in front of a young man with wide-set grey eyes who was holding the stump of his right arm against his chest and grinning. "Goddamn fucking Americans, never read their fucking orders, fucking fuckheads."

Bill kept going up the hill. The bombing was already over and Bill could hear the planes turn and return west. He watched them make a big circle overhead and disappear. Bill reached the top of the ridge where he had left Brownie. He looked across at the distant line of hills and he could see a German soldier standing, a dark figure against the sky, and he was laughing.

Brownie was stretched out on the ground. His legs were missing. Bill knelt down beside him and took his head in his lap. He put his hand on his chest to feel for a heart beat and then ran it down over his stomach and between his legs to try to stop the bleeding.

Brownie opened his eyes and lifted his head. He reached up and pulled Bill's face down toward his. "What does it all mean, Bill?" he whispered and a thin wash of blood trickled out of his mouth and down his chin.

Bill wiped the blood from Brownie's face. Bill looked up at the sky with his young old eyes. He stared up for a long time as if he could see something written there or maybe could see right through the dirty brown clouds of smoke and right up into heaven. "I'll tell you," he said at last. "It don't mean shit."

ELEVEN

I

I'VE GOT TO GET THESE MEN OUT OF MY ROOM. THEY ARE STACKED LIKE cordwood along one wall of the room so I can barely see the fucking poster.

I get out of bed and pick up a chair and systematically begin to bash their brains out. I start with the oldest. These are the most pathetic. They stand around with their penises in their hands, waiting to pee, and let me smack them in the face with the chair. Pretty soon, I am standing knee deep in blood and brains and little fragments of white bone. Luckily, the bodies crumble to dust as they fall and are blown away in the strong wind that is howling down out of the pass. Otherwise I wouldn't be able to move for the corpses.

The younger men give me a little more trouble, especially the ones with erections. They run around and try to hide like they have something important to do later on. I usually trap them up against the bed or find them behind the bathroom door frantically jerking off, trying to finish before I can hit them in the head. One of them comes all over my pyjamas and I hit him twice as hard and nearly tear his head right off so it tilts over at an impossible angle, grinning at me as his body slumps to the floor.

I am almost done now. There are only a few horny teenagers left. The doctor comes in the room and watches for a while but I threaten him with the chair and he leaves.

They are gone. I turn toward the poster and the calendar so I can finally figure out where the hell I am. There is a boy of eight standing there. He looks at me with wide-set grey eyes. I rush at him with the chair but he puts his hand against my chest and slides it down over my belly. When he puts it between my legs, I fall over on the bed and start to cry.

II

Today the teacher comes into the class and tells us that we are to go home. I don't know why but the teacher is crying.

Davy and I put on our jackets and go out to take the school bus home. Some of the older kids are shouting at each other and some of the girls are crying. Sister Mary makes us all say a prayer before the buses depart. We stand in the schoolyard in front of St. Ignatius and stand with our heads bowed while the principal leads us in prayer.

The bus takes about twenty minutes to get to our stop. Davy and I walk up the block to our house. We stand outside for a while but it is cold. The leaves are blowing off the trees. Almost all the trees are bare now. I want to go in and watch television.

As soon as I say it, Davy says he is going to go across the street and play. Davy never wants to do what I am doing. He hates that our parents dress us the same and that people sometimes can't tell us apart. He especially hates to be called Dougie. I like being called Davy but I would never tell him that because he would hit me. Sometimes I wish he'd let me be both of us.

I watch as Davy goes across the street to Jimmy's place. Jimmy is Davy's best friend and is the only one who can always tell us apart. Davy goes up to Jimmy's house but Jimmy's mom sends him away. Davy stands on their front porch and stares over at me watching him. Then he goes and sits in Jimmy's yard and plays with some toys that have been left out there. I go into the house.

My mom is sitting in the living room watching television. I like it that my mom is always home when I come home from school. But today my mom doesn't run up and hug me like she always does when I get home. She sits on the sofa in the living room and is crying. I have never seen my mom cry like this before. Sometimes she cries when she is angry or real happy but today she seems very sad.

I start to cry too even though I don't know why. I run over and throw my arms around my mom and she hugs me and cries even more.

We sit and watch the television together. A lot of people on the television are very upset. Some of them are angry and shouting and some of them are crying. They keep saying the same thing over and over.

Then they start to show the same thing over and over. It is a picture of a man in a car, with a woman and some other men. Then he suddenly falls forward onto the woman and another man is lying across the back of the car. I know that something bad has happened to this man, but I'm not sure what.

My mom is really crying now and I know that this man is very important. I look very closely when they next show the picture but I can see that it is not daddy. I don't think I ever met this man and they keep saying he is from Dallas. I don't know what part of Toronto Dallas is in.

The man on the television asks us to pray, so my mom and I get down in front of the picture of Jesus that hangs on the wall over the bookcase and we pray for a long time. I don't know what to pray for so I pray for a pony. After a while, I tug at my mom's sleeve because I want to ask her something and she gets real mad at me and yells and I start to cry so she hugs me and tells me she loves me.

I ask her what's wrong and she tells me the President has been shot. I ask her what president and she says it doesn't matter because he's a good man and Catholics everywhere have to pray that he's all right. So we pray some more.

Then they start to show the same thing on television again and I think that Davy would like to see this even if I am watching it. So I run outside to get him.

I fly around the boy's head. Don't go outside. Don't go outside, boy. Your brother doesn't want to see this. Dougie, leave your brother alone. Let him play. I fly faster and faster until everything is a blur except the boy running out into the yard. Please, let him play.

I call to Davy and he looks up at me and I tell him he's got to come quick or he'll miss it. He'll miss the man being shot.

When he hears about the man being shot, he jumps up and runs across the street without stopping to look. I watch the car come down the street. I watch it come down the street until it hits Davy and he goes flying up in the air and hits the windshield of the car and falls down on the pavement.

Davy doesn't move and I've never seen him hold his head like that, even though he can do some really neat tricks with his tongue. The car stops really fast and this tall man gets out of the car and runs back to Davy. I have to look twice to see that it's a man because he has really long brown hair. I've never seen hair like that before on a man. He bends down to look at Davy and then he looks over at me with these wide-set grey eyes.

I fly faster and faster around my head until I make a whirlwind which sucks me down into a single point of light.

My mom runs out of the house and stands in the road, screaming, *Davy!* My mother and I scream together.

III

Aminesis—the death of memory. Please. Aminesis—the death of memory. Please.

The doctor stands over the bed and puts his hand on my chest pushing me back against the bed. He looks at me with wide-set grey eyes and begins to cry. The tears drip down on me like rain.

"Only a little farther," he says. "A little bit farther."

The bright white light begins to blossom outside the window and he reaches up and closes my eyes.

TWELVE

I

BILLY GOT IN THE CAR AND DROVE OUT OF THE BIG PARKING LOT IN FRONT of the plant. He got onto the expressway and drove until he got to the turnoff that took him down to Bloor Street. He followed Bloor until he came to Jane. He turned north on Jane and drove for five minutes until he got to Simpson, then along Simpson to home.

He pulled up in front of the house and parked on the street. He had a club meeting to go to later on and would put the car in the garage after he got home. Billy Jr. was playing in the front yard and he and Billy tossed a ball back and forth for a few minutes before Billy went into the house for supper.

Violet was in the kitchen, listening to the radio while she put the finishing touches to supper. Billy came up behind her and slipped his hands around her waist. He leaned forward and nuzzled her neck and ran his hands up her body to cup her breasts. She wiggled her behind against him and laughed. She pushed his hands away as little Billy came into the kitchen.

Billy went over to the fridge and got a soda for his son and a beer for himself. He went into the living room and picked up the paper. It looked like Eisenhower was going to win the presidency in the States and Billy nodded to himself and smiled.

Billy looked around the living room and tried to decide where he would put the television. He had been putting away a little money from each paycheque and had planned to buy it for Christmas, but the union got them all a little bonus for signing the new contract, so he could buy it early. It would arrive on Saturday morning and he couldn't wait to see the look on little Billy Jr.'s face when he got back from Little League and it was there.

The dark man thought it would look good in the corner but Billy hardly ever listened to him anymore. He decided he would put it against the far wall away from the light of the window.

Billy got up and went into the backyard to look at the garden. The grass needed a little cutting, he thought. There were three crows flying in a circle over the house and he hoped they wouldn't eat the raspberries that grew along the back fence. He went back into the house.

Violet had had an accident with the gas oven and the inside of the kitchen was gutted and black. The side of Violet's head had been blown away and there were bits of white bone and drops of blood and bone spattered across the floor. Billy smiled at her and helped her clean it up and they sat down for supper.

II

Billy got up early Saturday morning and got in the shower. It was Violet's time of the month so he took an extra long shower and played with himself until his hand got sticky and wet. He looked down and saw that his hand was covered in blood. He rinsed off and got dressed.

He took Billy Jr. down to the park and watched while he played ball. He was sitting in the stands and was surprised to see a familiar face. It was Abel Baker, a name that Billy found very funny now that he'd been in the war. Abel told him that he still lived with Jonathon Cobb down in Colorado. Cobb had never really gotten over his daughter's death but didn't blame Billy for it anymore. Billy asked about Ephraim and Abel told him that his twin brother was now selling cars in Toronto. Billy promised to look him up the next time he was in the market for a car.

When they got back to the house, the new television had already arrived and Billy put it against the wall away from the window and turned it on. The reception was lousy and Billy finally had to put it in the corner like the dark man suggested. He looked around but the dark man wasn't there. When he turned on the television set the dark man appeared in a clown suit, laughing.

Billy Jr. stayed indoors all that day and Billy thought he could see some problems developing. The next day Billy Jr. didn't want to go to Sunday school. Billy was going to make him but Violet begged him to let the little tyke have fun for once and Billy finally laughed and relented. Billy Jr. watched the television all day until he finally fell asleep and Billy carried him up to bed.

He and Violet watched the television for a while longer. Then Violet kissed him on the mouth and slid her hands down his chest, across his belly, which was growing a little soft, and between his legs. After a bit she bent down and took him in her mouth until he finally got hard enough for them to fuck. They fucked for a while on the sofa, but Billy couldn't come so they stopped and went to bed.

III

Billy was floating in the air a few inches above the bed. He rolled over onto Violet but she pushed him off her. She turned away and closed her eyes. He reached over and twisted her head until he heard it crack. He left her lying there with her head turned on the pillow at an impossible angle.

He got up and walked down the hall toward the boy's room. The dark man was walking beside him and Billy reached out and took the dark man's hand in his. Billy pushed open the door of his son's room and walked over to the bed and looked down on the sleeping boy. He had kicked the blankets off in the night and was lying on top of the bare bed. Billy reached down and unbuttoned the boy's pyjama top and pulled down the bottoms until they were around his ankles.

The dark man took Billy's hand and placed it on the boy's chest and guided it down over his stomach and between his legs. Billy pulled his hand away and looked at it. It was blackened and scarred. Billy looked up at the dark man with pleading eyes but the dark man simply stared at him. Sarah and Alice were standing on the far side of the bed and they nodded for him to go on.

Billy leaned down and ran his tongue across his son's chest and down his belly to the small hairless crotch. He took the little cock in his mouth. The boy suddenly sat up in bed and pushed Billy's head away.

"What are you doing, daddy?" he asked. "What are you doing to me?" His son started to cry.

Billy looked around for the dark man and for Sarah and Alice but nobody was there. He pulled the blankets up over his son. "Nothing, Billy, nothing. Go back to sleep."

Bill looked at his right hand. There was light scarring on two fingers where he had been burned as a boy. He looked around the room.

The glow from the streetlight shimmered through the curtains into the room. The small room was painted light blue and had pictures of baseball players hanging on one wall. There was a small desk under the window with Billy Jr.'s homework piled neatly on top of it, ready for the morning. A small bookcase beside it had a few books and a baseball mitt on one shelf. The bed was narrow and made of maple. The little boy who lay in the bed looked up at him and was afraid.

William knew that something had really happened. He was afraid to go back to his bedroom because he might see his wife's pretty loving face twisted at an impossible angle.

He went downstairs and got the keys to the car. He took a can of gasoline out of the car and walked up to the house. He sprinkled the gas all around the house and up the walls as high as he could reach. He saved a little bit in the bottom of the can. He put the can to his mouth and took the gas in his mouth. He lit a match and held it at arm's length in front of him. He spit the gas in a perfect arch over the top of the match so the fireball hit the side of the house and exploded. He clamped his lips tight shut before the fire could come back and hit him in the face.

He got in the car and drove away.

THIRTEEN

I

HE HAS BEEN RUNNING FOR A LONG TIME. I WATCH HIM AS HE DRIVES down the dusty highway between the long rows of cacti. I could tell him that he doesn't need to run, that he did not set fire to his house three years ago in Toronto. I could tell him that his wife and son still love him and wonder where he is. I don't bother to try. He doesn't pay attention to voices anymore, no matter how loudly they scream in his ear.

I am floating in the clear desert sky, high above the car. If anyone other than the man in the car were here to see me they would think I was an eagle or, maybe, one of the legendary condor, drifting west from the Rocky Mountains. He might look up through the front window of his car and see me for what I really am, but this does not matter. As I said, he long ago stopped paying attention to angels.

It is beautiful here in the desert. The sun is bright and picks everything out in clean-cut detail. Red predominates but, there, a thin line of green marks the path of an underground river, the water flowing swift below the surface. Farther east, the direction the man is driving, the desert is covered by a thick layer of white sand, from which the region gets its name.

It is a long way from here to Toronto, where, not long from now, I lie beside my brother in my mother's womb, waiting to be born. It is so soon after our conception that our mother does not even know we are there yet. But I know. I sense my brother does not know and

I think that this is why, later, he will not want to do the things I do. He will know that we are not the same even though most people cannot tell us apart.

It is a long way from here to Toronto. It is even farther to the hospital in Edmonton, where I lie in a clean white bed, waiting for the new year to begin.

It is interesting to be three places at once. I enjoy looking down on the car as it speeds eastward through the desert toward our destiny. Behind the car, a narrow triangle of dust stretches back along the road for nearly half a mile. Here I am allowed to think in imperial measures. In 1955, nobody thought in metric except the Germans.

The car is old and does not run well. The man sometimes has trouble starting it in the morning and, often, it overheats in the desert sun. It is a deep emerald green although now it is coated in dust. The man bought it for twenty-five dollars in Tucson from a red-headed man named Steve. Steve got it from a Mexican in Nogales but this is not important. The car has no spare tire and the radio doesn't work. It doesn't work because the man smashed it with a tire iron as soon as he left Tucson. He thinks radio is a mind control device. He may be right. I don't know.

Back in Toronto, all there is to do is listen to my mother's heartbeat. It's pleasant to do that for a while but it loses its charm after an hour or two. In Edmonton there is even less to do for I am barely there at all anymore. The last few seconds of 1999 are ticking by and my mind is peeling away like the layers of an onion, sloughing off like the skin of one of the brightly-coloured rattlesnakes basking in the desert far below.

I look down on the man in the car and consider myself lucky. At least, my mind is still in one piece.

II

He drove down the narrow gravel road. He kept glancing in the rearview mirror. It was hard to see through the dust kicked up by the wheels of the car. He didn't think anyone was behind him but he couldn't be sure. They had a funny way of appearing and disappearing.

He looked over at the dark-clothed man in the passenger seat. The son of a bitch hadn't said a word since he picked him up on the highway just past Deming. It seemed like he had been driving for a long time.

At first he had simply drifted, driving from town to town. Ever since the fire that had stolen his wife and son away from him, he had wandered around looking for some understanding of what it all meant. "It doesn't mean shit," the dark man said when he finally spoke again.

It seemed aimless at first, but that was before he saw the pattern. When he traced his movements on a map, a pattern began to appear. It was all in code, of course. He didn't crack the code until he got to Tucson. Then it was simple. He bought the car and started driving east.

He looked up through the car window. That bird was there again. It had been there for days, flying right over the car. No matter how fast he moved it stayed with him. Whenever he stopped for gas or water or to pee in the bushes by the side of the road, the bird would fly in a tight perfect circle above the car. If he still had his gun, he would shoot it, but he had left his gun in Colorado a long time ago.

The road came to an end. There was a big sign that said "U.S. Army Testing Site. No Trespassing." Beyond the sign was a tall fence topped with barbed wire. He pulled the car over to the side of the road and drove along the fence for a while. Finally he came to a ravine. He stopped and got out of the car. The sides of the ravine were steep and covered with a thin layer of low spiky bush. He took his pack out of the car. He put it in gear and pushed it over the side of the ravine. It ploughed through the bush and came to a rest at the bottom of the slope. He tore up several of the bushes and threw them down on the car so that it was pretty well hidden.

He walked back toward the road dragging a spiny branch behind him to partly obliterate the marks of the car. The wind would do the rest.

He walked up to the fence and rattled it, curling the scarred fingers of his right hand around the wire and shaking it hard. Then he climbed up the side of the fence, throwing his coat over the barbed wire at the top to keep from being cut.

The dark man, who had been watching all of this from a seat on a large crumbling rock that sat at the edge of the great bank of sand, shook his head, laughed and walked back down the road toward Deming.

He watched the dark man until he was out of sight and then turned away and walked across the desert toward its centre.

III

I am rushing now from place to place to place. I cannot decide where I want to be when the moment comes.

In Edmonton, the light through the window is getting brighter and brighter as the micro-seconds tick down to midnight. The young doctor with the long brown hair and grey eyes is standing silhouetted in the window and I am afraid for him. He turns and winks at me.

In Toronto, my cells are joining together, reducing from two thousand and forty-eight on down to one thousand and twenty-four and then to five hundred and twelve and so on down to one single fertilized egg, when my brother and I will be finally and completely united and the same. At the final instant my father's sperm will leap away from the egg and swim back down my mother's uterus and into her vagina to be sucked back into my father's penis as he unorgasms.

Because it is my parents, I use all the proper medical terms. It is not important anyway for all that matters to me is the moment of conception/deconception.

I decide to spend my last few moments watching the man. I have found as the process of aminesis proceeds that I much prefer to watch others than to watch myself.

The man is standing on a flat glassy plain. He has long since absorbed enough radiation to kill him but he has not fallen down yet. The Army, if it knew, would have mixed feelings about his presence. He is, of course, intruding on one of their most holy rituals. On the other hand, they would relish the opportunity to observe close-up the effects of a thermonuclear device on human flesh. As it turns out they could have their cake and eat it, too. Isn't the punishment for blasphemy burning at the stake? It is a pity they do not know he is here.

He stood on the edge of the glassy plain. In the distance he could see a tower of metal. There was no one here now. No one dared come here, not even the dark man. There was only him. And that funny bird that flew in slow perfect circles above his head. He waved to the bird and he thought it waved back.

The man waves at me and I wave back. I have forgotten I am a bird and the gesture sends me spiralling lower. In Edmonton, the light is now unbearable, while in Toronto, the egg sits in a sea of forgotten and frustrated sperm, its walls growing thinner and thinner. My brother and I are one. Here, I am a bird with wings of flame.

He took a deep breath. There was a moment of silence. *"Our Father who art . . . "* His breath was sucked from his lungs and there was an instant of total silence. He reached out with his right hand and then the fire hit his face and through the flames he could see his entire arm was ablaze and at last he was clean again as the bird flew down out of the sky and joined with him like a phoenix.

The sperm flies from the egg.

The window explodes in a shower of glass and heat. The room is filled with flames and the stares of wide-set grey eyes.

A Note on the 3-Day Novel-Writing Contest

The **Anvil Press International 3-Day Novel Contest** (formerly sponsored by Pulp Press), the world's most infamous literary marathon, takes place during the Labour Day weekend (the weekend of the first Monday in September) on typewriters and word processors around the world. As the new sponsors of this uniquely Canadian phenomenon, we are thoroughly convinced of the contest's value and importance to writers of long fiction, and remain confident that future contests will discover other fine talents waiting for a suitable challenge.

The rules are simple: entrants, having filled out a registration form and paid the entry fee, begin writing at 12:01 a.m. Saturday, and must stop at or before 12 midnight Monday. The novels may be written in any location and using whatever method, so long as the writing takes place during the three prescribed days. If you cannot type, or do not have access to a typewriter or computer, you are permitted to have your handwritten novel typed during the week following the contest. Entrants then return their finished novels (except handwritten manuscripts) to Anvil Press sometime during the week following the contest, accompanied by a self-addressed stamped envelope and a statement by a witness confirming the novel's completion over the Labour Day Weekend. The winner is announced October 31.

First prize is publication and instant notoriety.

For registration forms and/or more information, send a self-addressed stamped envelope (or $1.00 if outside Canada, as non-Canadian stamps are not useable) to:

>3-Day Novel Contest
>Anvil Press Publishers
>#15 – 2414 Main Street
>Vancouver, B.C. canada v5t 3e3
>ph: (604) 876-8710

Write for a free catalogue of other Anvil Press books and pamphlets!